Memories of Lazarus

The Texas Pan American Series

memories of Lazarus

BY ADONIAS FILHO

Translated by FRED P. ELLISON

DRAWINGS BY ENRICO BIANCO

UNIVERSITY OF TEXAS PRESS, AUSTIN

The Texas Pan American Series is published with the assistance of a revolving publication fund established by the Pan American Sulphur Company and other friends of Latin America in Texas. Publication of this book was also assisted by a grant from the Rockefeller Foundation through the Latin American translation program of the Association of American University Presses.

ISBN 978-0-292-75021-0
Library of Congress Catalog Card No. 77–75500
Type set by G&S Typesetters, Austin
Printed by The University of Texas Printing Division, Austin
Bound by Universal Bookbindery, Inc., San Antonio

TO ROSITA

Introduction

One of Brazil's outstanding novelists of the postwar era, Adonias Filho is also a respected leader among its intellectuals. In the last twenty-five years he has produced four novels and a collection of *novelas*, along with extensive critical writings of major importance. He represents the generation that arose after 1945 in Brazil (as in other parts of the world), advocating experimentation in writing and a more aesthetically oriented literary art. Regionalism and the situation of man in society remain important to him, however, and in his novels he has shown a very Brazilian sense of accommodation of these concerns to the newer aestheticism in art. He later assumed the editorship of a big Rio de Janeiro newspaper and became a publisher, politician and political writer, translator, and, with increasing success, novelist and critic, earning recognition in the form of membership in the Brazilian Academy of Letters and in the post of Director of Brazil's National Library. His novels are now beginning to be translated abroad.

Adonias Filho is the almost exclusively used pen name of Adonias Aguiar Filho — "Filho" indicates that his father, a cacao plantation owner, had the same name before him. He was born in southern Bahia on November 27, 1915, in the municipality of Ilheus, parts of which were at that time still a wilderness. Much of his fiction has dealt with this area and the nearby "Itajuipe Territory," which is becoming synonymous with the isolation, primitiveness, and violence that the author found in its humid cacao groves, rain forests and, farther inland, arid tablelands, valleys, and mountains. His early schooling was acquired in Ilheus, the cacao port, and later in Salvador, the old colonial capital, now bypassed but still an ideal place for the young man to learn Brazilian history, read the national literature, and meditate on the destinies of his native land. It was also the place he began his literary and journalistic careers—in Brazil, for economic reasons, these are often linked—and completed his formal education.

In 1936 he moved to the capital at Rio to continue his literary career. Working as a newspaperman and contributor to literary journals, Adonias Filho met and collaborated in those agitated days with writers of many different political and literary persuasions. He worked with two of the Catholic modernists, Tasso da Silveira and Andrade Muricy, the strange self-probing "psychological" novelists and innovators Cornelio Pena and Lucio Cardoso, the novelist of social panorama Otavio de Faria, and had as a close friend the "northeastern" novelist Rachel de Queiroz, who, with José Lins do Rego, Graciliano Ramos, and Jorge Amado, were dominating the novel with their intensely social and realistic art.

Though no critic has understood the value of the telluric in Brazilian literature better than he, Adonias Filho's own evolution led away from realism: "I continue to believe too much in man, and in the possibilities of his intelligence, to accept reality as the life blood of the modern novel"—reality is various and changing, and there is something in man that is superior to it. In the mid-thirties he tore up a documentary novel he had written and rejected another that he was later to rewrite and publish under the almost untranslatable title of *Corpo Vivo* (perhaps *Cajango*, the name of its lively hero, would be acceptable) in

1962. He had also begun to think of another work in his "cacao cycle," but it was not to reach definitive form until 1952, as the present *Memórias de Lázaro* (*Memories of Lazarus*). Part of the same cycle and perhaps the least notable artistically, *Os Servos da Morte* (*Servants of Death*) was the first of his novels to be published, in 1946.

The end of World War II, in which Brazil participated actively, brought significant changes in political, social, and intellectual life, especially in the direction of greater individual freedom. A new literary generation had arisen, the so-called generation of 1945, which was vanguardist, experimental, and interested in the implications of modern art for literature. Joyce, Proust, Kafka, Virginia Woolf, and later the French writers of the *nouveau roman* were major influences; so, particularly for Adonias Filho, were Faulkner, Jouhandeau, Jacob Wasserman, Henry James, and Hermann Hesse's *Steppenwolf*. Adonias Filho has been one of the leaders of the new movement, along with Clarice Lispector, whose first novel had appeared in 1944, and João Guimarães Rosa, whose first collection of short stories was published in 1946. Other important novelists of the new orientation are Geraldo Ferraz, Rosario Fusco, and Maria Alice Barroso.

Through the example of his own novels as well as his critical writings, Adonias Filho has done much to further what he has called the "structural revolution"—the re-awakened interest in language for its own sake and new approaches to character development, the handling of space and time, and narrative technique generally. For him, "technique is that which makes possible the clearest understanding of human problems and, in the most subjective way, the psychological delineation of character." Adonias Filho saw technical experimentation as the means for renewing Brazilian literature. The latter he considers to have arisen in the mid-nineteenth century, after three hundred years of "fermentation" in the form of oral literature, principally religious plays and folk tales, which subsequently influenced more sophisticated forms of drama and fiction. The documentary basis of literature has always been strong in Brazil, but literary conventions—of style, for example—have also shaped fiction. Regionalism has persisted and been given new impetus by the modernist movement of the nineteen-twenties, which, through poetry, and out of respect for the vernacular, freed the literary language from many of its restraints. After 1930, a renaissance occurred in modern fiction, which, without turning its back on folklore, gave supreme value to "Brasiliana."

In the summer of 1967, in Austin, I had the great pleasure of chatting with the author about his views on literature, especially about the regional basis of *Memories of Lazarus*. He made it clear that the Ouro Valley actually exists, in the hinterlands beyond Itajuipe and Coaraci. "Of course," he added, "it is half truth and half a dream." Under many influences, including Shakespeare's *Midsummer Night's Dream* and certain of the mystery tales of Poe, the valley was transformed. Although he visited the area as a young man, most of the episodes came from his own fantasy. Nor does the novel make any sociological affirmations.

The Ouro Valley is disquieting, if not terrifying, in its strangeness. Since specific links with reality are often dissolved, Alexandre's narration quickly transcends the local; time becomes a function of his hallucinations. In creating the Ouro Valley, its look, its atmosphere, its inner "feel," Adonias Filho has eliminated all but a few specific features—for example, the slough, the searing wind, Jeronimo's cavern, the dusty road, the earth's hot crust, the black sky. Men are described with a similar laconism in their simple lives and in their primitive society. As a matter of technique, Adonias Filho has depended upon the observation of gesture, facial expression, or other movement to convey inner states and upon a few physical details to establish outward appearance. Constant repetition of these details serves to give an almost sculptural quality to his characters. The author is "visual without being a landscape painter," in the words of Rachel de Queiroz, speaking of Adonias Filho's newest work, *Léguas da Promissão* (*Promised Leagues*, 1968), a collection of tales of the same Itajuipe Territory.

The author has created an original literary style. Unlike Guimarães Rosa, who invented a sometimes impenetrable idiom for his stories of the hinterland of Minas Gerais, Adonias Filho stays within the bounds of the Portuguese language of Brazil. He creates through subtle syntactical rhythms that depend, in many instances, on balanced elements, ellipses without verbs, simple short bursts of words, frequently with a ternary rhythm. The critic Sergio Milliet has remarked on its musicality, "which is simple and full like a chant or a Biblical verse." Indeed, *Memories of Lazarus*, in the original, and hopefully in the translation, demands to be read aloud. When Jeronimo, who is illiterate, speaks, there is no disruption of the stylistic unity; we are merely told that "his language was naturally coarser and his turn of phrase poorer" than the language of the narrator. The author is thus left free to use language as creatively as possible.

Memories of Lazarus is rich in themes, whether of the locality, the national culture, or the world at large. Merely a few examples, at the regional level, are cacao cultivation and backlands ranching as styles of life, and in a limited sense the cyclic drought, with its tragic social implications. These might also be viewed as themes of national import, and indeed they have been thus presented in earlier northeastern novels. An especially productive national (or even continent-wide) theme is the conflict between the littoral, with its cities, and the relatively uncivilized hinterlands. Probably it is the universal level of interpretation of themes, theses, and symbols that gives the novel its widest appeal. One may recognize men of all times and all places, who have been stripped of every vestige of civilization and reduced to their most elemental humanity—remembering the beautiful wild horses of the Ouro Valley, one hesitates to say "animality."

Among Adonias Filho's works, *Memories of Lazarus* has already been singled out as a modern-day masterpiece. To many who are versed in nineteenth-century Brazilian literature, it cannot but recall a very different and yet in so many important ways similar book—the classic *Dom Casmurro* (available in English under the same title) by Machado de Assis. Not only is there the same profound knowledge of man but also the same preoccupation with the tragic limitations upon the human capacity to discover truth. The brutalized Rosalia and the darling Capitu are, ultimately, sisters.

F. P. E.

Memories of Lazarus

INFINITE IS THE ROAD WITH ITS CURVES, its hills, and its trees. It is no ordinary road, with birds and a verge of grass, but a sinuous line on the red, dry earth. Where it begins, no one knows. Nor where it ends. To those who have known it as we have, since childhood, it is as intimate as the crude objects in primitive huts. It seems almost human. It allows us on it with scorn; it is insensible, without a trace of kindness. Were we blinded we could easily find every cactus that attacks us; were we to lose our sense of touch we would have no trouble saying which of its stones is hardest. To those others, those travelers who by some miracle have gone along it without ever breaking open its secrets, it would be just another road.

For us, who live in the valley and keep it clean every day with our feet, who bear the sun and tolerate the rain as we walk upon it, it is the world in which our lives are linked and our hopes and sufferings are joined. So often, like a snake, it divides into a thousand different trails. It penetrates the plateaus, invades the empty unexpanding landscape compressed within the monotony of the tablelands. It is not held back by the devastated pastures, by the earth eroded by heavy rains. To tell the truth, I think the valley exists because the road exists. Everything—men and thatched huts, desires and hatreds—is concentrated around the roadbed like a body around its spine.

The cattle, the sheep, the pigs, the planted fields, would not have come. Nor would the first inhabitants have come. Even the muddy slough, once perhaps a meek and narrow river, and now a deep bed of mire and stagnant water, would not have become as it is, sticky, vile-smelling, polluted. The very earth, still uncultivated and ember-red, would not have lost its cover of rock, its crust of sandpaper, its desert look. The clouds would have been different, and the sky, that enormous true mirror, would not have reflected as it does the harshness of the earth, with its huge scalelike rocks.

But the road, too much alive, is for the valley like its very heart. It orients the sick and the drunk, the dogs that are famished and outcast. No force on earth, either in or outside the valley, can undo its evil destiny—and no spell on earth can obscure its presence, the trajectory it imposes, that line without a beginning that widens at the very point where the water turns brackish. The scarcity of water, which seems to evaporate in the depleted air, forces an appalling aridity on the pastures. But the cattle have clean hides and in the foothills never stray far from the huts. The valley floor is almost like lava that never quite cooled, but that which characterizes it even more universally is the shifting wind.

Constant and strong, almost wild, to it I attribute everything that happens there that is violent and sorrowful. It whips the scorched grass, scourges the livestock, and doesn't even spare the dust on the road. That is why we always keep our windows closed. And that is why the corrals are made of thick, heavy wood. Torturing the plain day and night, almost like a live demon, it seems to have chosen, among all the zones of the earth, to make its rounds in just this valley. It keeps you from hearing the sound of horses passing on the road, the crack of whips, the angry shouts. A persistent murmuring that seems to be the only voice in the valley.

Probably it comes from the mountains. Down across the plain, like an echo, one might say, from the gorge that separates the valley and mountain, its sound is neither harsh nor hoarse. A lament that startles, that stretches each nerve. As a child I loved it. Afterward I hated it. Today, I could not understand the valley, and I swear to you I could not even think of the road, without these blasts. Passing always and never ceasing to pass, it leaves its mark on everything like a stigma, on grass as on stones, on birds as on trees, on dirt as on men.

Especially on men. Here, though girls sing at harvest and boys shout as they break colts, black is the soul and brutish the heart. And men are not tormented by the fear of being destroyed by fellow men or by the need for physical strength to keep from being devoured in the pitiless fight. Here the weak die at their mothers' breasts. The sick are cut off, rot, are naturally eliminated. Brutish and insensible, only the savages remain, and they are consumed with hatred. Clinging to the crust of the valley like prisoners, like caged animals on a lightless plain, they nonetheless reflect, in the anguish of their blood, the panic of darkness and solitude. Their community is, however, quite old. Generation has followed generation upon this same land, planting and gathering, watching over herds and flocks. This almost primitive life continually narrows—from the valley to the farm, from the farm to the road, from the road to the yard, from the yard to the house.

Always the same color as the earth, their houses, like lanterns swaying to and fro in the dark, seem to resist the broader world that surrounds the valley. Beyond are uninhabited forests, high mountains that limit the landscape, perhaps vast open prairies, groves of trees that fail to soften the solitude. Heavy and slow, clouds that move southward challenge our imagination and our curiosity. Even farther, lost in distances the eye cannot reach, perhaps there lies, at the end of the road, the real world that my father, Abilio, used to speak of. My father and Jeronimo's great friend.

PART ONE

INSIDE THE CAVERN IN THE ROCKS, his entire body in somber relief, Jeronimo is speaking. I see him as distinctly as before. His fat cheeks, thick lips, bull neck. His long black hair, partly plaited, that reaches to his shoulders. His smooth broad forehead, and his flattened nose. Large mustaches about his mouth. His steady voice takes on weight, pours out into the cavern air like breath. Enormous arms are crossed on his hairy, muscular, herculean chest. Controlling my desire to shout, containing my restlessness, outwardly displaying a certain serenity, I am afraid he will get up and that, in the partial light, his face will become contorted. But on the dirt floor, between stones, wood is feeding the fire. It illuminates his face, which had shown surprise but now is impassive, devoid of reaction. With his back against a large flat rock, he is speaking, his words like slivers of an incomplete recollection:

"I don't know why you came back, Alexandre. I swore a thousand times, to everyone in the valley, that you would not come back. When you left, they all came here the next afternoon. They were excited, some were carrying tools, some were shaking their fists, and everybody was shouting: 'We want Alexandre!' I spread my arms, blocking the entrance with my body, and, ready for anything, cried out: 'Alexandre has fled; he has left the valley for the rest of his life!' Whether because they feared me or believed me, they withdrew in silence."

Pausing, as if wishing to recompose certain details, Jeronimo brings his lips together. He stoops down, arranging the wood, and blows on the fire. His gaze, which reflects the flames, is so clear that he seems not to see at all. He gets up, huge, a giant, without showing the least curiosity. And he continues, in quiet tones, chewing his tobacco:

"You shouldn't have come back, Alexandre. Here in the valley men are worse than beasts. Wild horses are the humane ones in this valley."

Jeronimo stops, the warmth of the coals upon his feet, and he almost doesn't breathe. I know the wind is blowing outside. There is the starless painful sky, like a mantle of lead. In the pastures, no one. Deserted, lost in darkness, the road will reveal nothing. At this moment, the valley is a dead zone. All doors are shut, all windows closed. Safe from the wind and the dark, people will not suppose that I, Alexandre, am once more among them. I stand up, under Jeronimo's vigilant gaze, and reveal my decision:

"I don't know either why I came back, Jeronimo. At Nathanael's house, when Nathanael died, I had a feeling that I would come back."

Explaining further:

"I didn't just come back, Jeronimo. Something brought me."

Jeronimo does not understand. But, opening his arms wide, as the firelight makes our faces seem harder, he exclaims, in an effort to understand:

"The valley, the spirit of the valley!"

Were it in his power, he would not let me leave. It's true there is the cover of night, but there are people who can see in the dark. Above all, despite the passing of time, the valley still has not forgotten. My land abandoned, the crops lost, the cattle turned loose—all this has become a powerful reminder in the valley. They shifted the weight of their punishment to my land, to a piece of my own body. The land answered for my absence. And Jeronimo is not unaware of all this.

While he is once more bending over the fire to blow on the coals, with the smell of roast meat permeating the air, I step quickly away and, picking up his lantern, look for the door. Only his voice rises and I hear his question:

"Are you going to look for your house? Your house, Alexandre —" but he does not finish the sentence.

As always, however, comes his wish:

"The powers of fortune go with you."

I force the door open, feel the wind cut my face, hear its wild howl. My feet are bare. Jeronimo's leather breeches fill out my flanks. Jeronimo himself has already cleansed my wounds. Since I arrived and since the moment when Jeronimo asked, "Why did you come back," a night and a day have passed. The warmth of the fire has already fortified my heart; Jeronimo has already said and repeated that the valley is ever the same, indomitable and free, brutal and cruel. Nothing has happened in my absence, nothing except that the older of the two Luna brothers has killed the other with a knife. Sitting on his haunches, Jeronimo is tearing roasted meat off the iron spit itself with his teeth. I close the door, leave Jeronimo's cavern behind, and then the road accepts me. The old road, however, is not the same.

I know that I shall walk it for a long time tonight. Though in the valley, my farm lies miles beyond Jeronimo's place. To reach it, I shall have to pass other farms, go by the leper's shack, outbrave a strip of forest. I am saved meanwhile by the certainty that the road is mine, no less mine than the darkness or my own heart. But, acknowledging the road and advancing over it, I cannot escape the mastery that the valley exerts over all its people. Not even the stars have light. Black, dense clouds cover up the sky and cut off all horizons. The sparse houses, closed up like tombs, look empty. My own footfalls, my labored breathing, above all my eyes exhausted from peering. Bats fly squeaking and struggle against the wheeling wind. A little more, a little more, and I shall find the leper's shack.

Follow me, please. Follow me and ask no questions. That deformed shred of a man, who used to be called Gemar Quinto and who now is only a skeleton, might hear us. If he gets curious, he may open the window or rise up out of the night, enveloped in the muffled sound of wings, like a horrible apparition. I have seen him often in times past—and I know how terrible it is to look for his eyes in a face that is a lumpy mass of discolored splotches. His puffy lips will try to speak, his hands will reach, as usual, for the stumps of his ears. Follow me, then, in silence.

This is his shack. He himself built it years ago, when they

drove him out and his dogs were killed. He came alone and alone cut down the trees, sawed the beams, prepared the clay. It is crude, poor, sad, but it is his. Here he lived out the remaining days. As you know, the water hole is not far away, and there was never cleaner water to wash a condemned body and to calm poisoned blood.

Beyond the water hole, the strip of forest. I do not know by what magic it is sustained in the valley, which is as dry, unrelenting, and forbidding as a desert. Among its trees, deep in shadows that haunt me, I feel as if I were a child again—when I used to walk through it, with Jeronimo, gripped by a strange fascination that almost took my breath away. The old sensations come back to me, a rhythmless kind of music, subduing the wind, voices that shout and stop dead still under the weight of strangled sounds. To me, this is still an enchanted forest. Invisible creatures, gay and noisy, leap across the grass, and I fear they will snatch away my lantern.

There, beyond the first curve in the road, I shall find the farm gate. Don't talk to me, I beg you. Don't, because, from the moment Jeronimo left me at the foot of the mountain, I have always wondered if it would be possible to return. In the heart of the forest, at Terto's side; in the village; even at Nathanael's house, I always thought of coming back to tarry in front of this gate. But, though I have my lantern lit, I look in vain for the markers that Jeronimo set in the ground, and, by raising the light, I can see that the fence stakes have been burned. They were here—and this is what Jeronimo hid from me—they burned down my place. With my blood circulating like liquid fire within me, with eyes moist, I try to imagine how the torches were hurled. Probably they came when they saw us, Jeronimo and me, head for the mountain. I wonder if they brought Roberto's body, all dirty and bloody? Had they already buried it when they came? They did not go into the house, I imagine. They gathered dry branches, piled up wood, touched off the fires. From a distance they watched the fire as it struggled with the wind, the smoke rising and spreading over the valley.

If you wish, you can all turn around, keep to the right, climb the first slope, and watch. You will not see me, for my body is indistinguishable in the dark, but you will see the lantern running among the bushes. Gripping it in my fingers, as if my hand were a claw, I don't even see its light. I go forward, stumbling, and, when I stop, I immediately make out the walls. Come, come quickly and I'll show them to you!

I set the lantern on the ground, right where the porch was, and breathe the thin air of the valley. But for the wind, and, also, the excitement of my memory, my nerves would perhaps have quieted, giving way to a less irascible feeling. Beyond the wind and my memory, however, comes the first blackened wall, the mark of fire upon its bricks. Farther on, another. And after that, still others. It is an open enclosure, with isolated columns standing up like men. In the open area that they delimit and that to me is like an exposed stomach, there survives, imprisoned, a world that I am not sure can ever be mine again. The desolation within does not frighten me and, once more holding up the lantern, I enclose myself between the walls that Jeronimo helped to build. I observe that the fire has consumed everything, furniture and clothing, doors and roof—has consumed everything, I repeat, except the fantastic walls that are revealed to me in the circle of light and are unsuspected in the nocturnal darkness.

Meanwhile, even though my blood flows normally in my veins,

even though all my instinctive violence is gone, I can tell you that I have not to this moment lost my look of utter desperation. My burning eyes deform the light itself. My lips, which should have shouted a curse, are drawn tight as if to repress emotion. Suddenly the energy that brought me ceases. The spell that forced my return to the valley is broken. Before I begin to hear Rosalia's voice, however, and once more see her eyes dancing in the darkness, before these walls start to fall and night itself starts to fade, I think of running away. Of hurling myself headlong once again, I know not where. To escape like a man eternally a loser, with no one to give him rest or shelter, hopelessly exhausted and beaten. Were it not for this final fascination —digging into my own self, as if for buried treasure, in the ashes of this fire—were it not for the silly wish to hold the past in my hands, I would not wait for the morning sun. Unexplainable, the imperative that dominates me. Nerves, conscience, flesh, these are not dead pieces of me but are slaves to a confession that should never be made. The interior roots of what still may be a human mind are like soggy feet. They hurt my bones, they tread on my inner being. They walk with careful, measured steps amid the harrowing noise of wheels, as of a heavy carriage on an endless desert of sand.

Not the least sense of panic. I hadn't known it earlier, on other occasions, nor do I feel it now that I know everything is coming to an end. Through Jeronimo's voice, my father, Abilio, left me the way, the marvelous way, the way of freedom that neither wounds nor wearies. And I shall travel it, like my father, long, long before the valley awakens. There is still time for the past to approach. Plenty of time for it to reverberate, like an echo, down in the valley.

Impossible to say where my body was taking me; sustained by its blood but inwardly unconscious and lifeless, it was autonomous, as if I myself had departed. If a dead body could move, it would act as mine did, now that the great rocky plain had been surmounted. There were a good many painful moments before my astonished eyes could become aware of the boggy earth. Thanks to the wind, I was finally able to see thick, low-flying clouds. Struggling over the slippery bottom, still murky and unknown, I thought to myself that the valley had been left behind. The trees were altogether different. Overrun by weeds, destroyed by rank vegetation, the road was no longer at hand. I had surely wandered into an unknown world.

Mastering the wind and the cold, however, and extinguishing within me what had been desire and hatred, I was left with only my urge for self-preservation. I raised my hands to my face, impelled as if by a defensive instinct, and once more lifted up my eyes. Still dazed, it was only by a tremendous effort that I managed to keep my feet, though gasping and shaking. Very slowly, as the rain drenched my face, reason recovered strength and images began to return to equilibrium. I saw the bed, the bed and the mattress, both as vile as the sheet. The pail and the clay basin, the huge leather suitcase. And, the only living thing left, myself.

Hurting like Gemar Quinto's, my hands splashed in the marsh waters, one violently rubbing the other, like strange fighting fish. Had Jeronimo been there, he would have said:

"Alexandre, your hands are as hard as hooves."

Truly, two monstrous hands, coarse, hardened, used to the axe and to the work that farm and cattle demand. Looking at them, I could feel my worried eyes come to rest upon my fingers, which had so often been so near and yet so far from what might be considered Rosalia's suffering. Merely a name but now that my memory had receded so much, someone said, inside me, vehemently:

"Rosalia will not like this house."

It was Jeronimo. He was then helping me raise the walls of my house. Naked from the waist up, barefoot, chewing tobacco, he looked like the man I had always known. He leaned over the handle of his hoe and, observing me as if I were a stranger, concluded:

"The Ouro Valley ends here. Over there, in that slough, the late Abilio, your father, met his death."

Drawing closer to Jeronimo, who for the first time was speaking so freely of my father, I pressed my memory still more. Descending, submerging in a quick deep plunge, I was able to glimpse again, as if through waves, the final face of my father, Abilio. He had had other faces, in his life, all of them having been transformed into this one face that, at last was stilled in the bowels of death. Impossible to forget his square jaw, his sharp teeth, his black beard, his pallor. Deep sockets seemed to be shielding his tired eyes. Pulled up to his neck, the canvas sheet hid the rest of his body—I knew of course that his arms and legs, his chest and abdomen were mutilated. That was the final and most powerful image of my father.

Moving his hoe, which was mixing the clay, Jeronimo brought me back to reality; shutting off my private recollections, I could see the bricks made by Canuto, in the factory in the valley. I sat down on them and sensed that someone, speaking through my lips, was asking Jeronimo:

"You must tell what happened, Jeronimo."

He stopped the motion of his arms and, once more leaning his body over the hoe handle, began to talk. Listen, I beg you. Listen and believe, because Jeronimo does not lie.

"You should have known Abilio, Alexandre. The sort who spoke with his eyes and in them reflected a savage hatred. When I met him for the first time, he was still young. He had run off from Ilheus, I was told, because the city was too much for him, rejected as he was by everyone there and with his mother forced to live in a house of prostitution. Despised, homeless, he tried in vain to learn who his father was. He could have been this man or that one; the owner of the store where he worked or the cacao planter who was having his shoes shined—actually, his father could have been anybody, even Alfredo the idiot, or Ernesto the thief. There was always the sea, Abilio used to say, but the sea was not enough to take away the reality of a mother, now aged and feeble-minded, who waited on prostitutes like a slave.

"I don't know Ilheus, Alexandre, and I don't know the sea either. I was born in the valley, have grown up and lived here to this day. I know what the valley is, its wind, its sky, its people. But, had I been Abilio, I likewise would not have hesitated a moment to trade Ilheus for the valley. Here, at least, there is solitude. And Abilio, your father, loved solitude. He was a man withdrawn, Alexandre. A man withdrawn like Gemar Quinto.

"In one conversation after another, Abilio would always tell how he ran away. At the time he was working with João Garganta, the water vendor. Confidently the customers would wait for them every morning. They came from a long way off, from Malhado, driving the little burro that carried the barrels. No doubt it was a joy to see the water flow and hear the sound of it pouring into the jugs. João Garganta, with his vile temper, treated him brutally and shouted at him. Day after day, at work, Abilio planned his escape. First, however, he must say good-by to his mother. Above all, he had to find money.

"Whether he got to say good-by to his mother, I don't know. Whether he managed to find money, I also don't know. However, I know that, at that time, Englishmen were in Ilheus to build a railroad. They were hiring men to clear the jungle, cut trees, make crossties. Abilio was taken on with the gang that was headed for the Almada region. Abilio used to recall his comrades, one by one, and finally exclaim, 'A pack of wolves, all of them!' Entombed in the forest, nearly naked and always armed, they were forever fighting, and rare was the time when one's best friend of today did not turn into his worst enemy tomorrow. As in the valley, Alexandre, those who stayed alive were the ones who knew how to hit hardest, how to kill fastest. The English-men did not come in person but merely sent orders, from afar. Getting longer and longer, advancing at a bloody cost, the rail-road kept recruiting the scum of villages and farms. Abilio was able to stand it until the day the stonemasons appeared. They came from Ilheus and were better paid.

"All of them knew Abilio's mother and, in their spare time, would amuse themselves by provoking the youth. 'A nightmare!' I recall Abilio's exclaiming. Feeling that it would be impossible to remain, that it would be impossible to live with his open wound, he left with no particular destination, as yet unaware of the existence of the valley. But whether he wished it or not, Abilio would have to come face to face with the valley. Thus it was that, from trail to trail, almost exhausted by his journeys, he crossed the mountains and stopped, on the road down there.

"I remember it well, Alexandre. The valley people, isolated

from the world, living like a tribe, could not contain their astonishment. I can still see the late Borges' face, already emaciated by his disease, as he cried out: 'No one knows him!' Someone no one knew who was coming to stay. Divided up long ago, the land in the valley already had owners. You know, Alexandre, that land here is more than a piece of ground. It becomes a part of the human body like nerves and blood. Land, Alexandre, is as important as a woman.

"A man with no land, like Abilio, was a threat. It would be risky to stay and not have a patch of kale or a clump of grass for his horse. It was then that, to everyone's surprise, I invited him to work in my field. Abilio arrived with only the clothes on his back. He brought a sadness with him, Alexandre. A spirit that had kept alive solely because it hated everything—and I can say that Abilio hated even me, Jeronimo, his friend.

"But everyone in the valley was like Abilio. Everyone, Alexandre, I swear it. A happy person, someone who has never had a blight on him, will not live here. He will flee in fear of the blackness of the sky, the loneliness of this valley that is slowly being strangled by the crazy wind. Abilio stayed in the valley, he later told me, because the valley is not of this world. A realm forgotten as he used to explain it, where men are the more human because they are not afraid of pain, of fear, and do not hide their anger. 'You people in the valley are alive at least.'— I shall never forget Abilio's words.

"It was when he came into my cavern, his beard heavy and his chest heaving beneath his ragged clothes, that I felt how uncouth I was. With the fire reflecting in his eyes, for his gaze was strong and hard, Abilio convinced me of an amazing thing: I must have had a father and a mother. Others, preceding me, explained my origins. Even today, Alexandre, after so many

years, I don't understand very well. I know, however, that before
Abilio, I thought about nothing but tilling the earth with my
hands and had no feelings beyond weariness, hunger, and thirst.
It was Abilio who developed my mind, I am sure. I learned to
protect myself, and only after he came did I perceive the solitude
in which I lived. I felt the need to abandon my silence and then
I began to visit the late Borges. Then after Borges', João Cardoso's house. You did not know João Cardoso, Alexandre, but
you have heard his name many times. João Cardoso's house was
down there where the tallest cactus lines the road.

"He was the oldest man in the valley, Alexandre. He was
miserly and deaf, and, to see him from a distance, no one would
have said that João Cardoso was full grown. I remember him, his
long hair tangled in his beard, his dwarfed stature, his shriveled
body that was already bent and trembling. He went barefooted
like all the rest of us, his speech coming with a wheezing sound,
his hands hardly able to work the leather. He lived with Paula in
the back part of the house. To tell the truth, the house was a
vile-looking shack, and no one could explain how it stood up
against the wind. In the front was the shop—if one can call that
enormous room a shop, with its wooden counter, piled high with
sole leather, ropes, saddles, and cinches. In the back, there were
two rooms. To this day I don't know which of the two was
Paula's.

"Abilio began to frequent the shop along with me. He didn't
drink or smoke, but he liked to chat with the old man. For lack
of time, because I was building a new pen for the pigs, I quit
going to the shop. Abilio, however, kept on. For days, weeks,
months, until a storm came. A deluge, Alexandre, I remember it
well. The wind blew furiously, as night fell in the midst of day,
as the sky seemed to burst in lightning above us. Lying on the

floor of my cave, thinking of Abilio, I counted the minutes, the minutes and the thunder claps. When the thunder stopped, with the rain still beating down, I set out running in the direction of the shop. I was pretty sure that Abilio was with João Cardoso.

"I was not mistaken, Alexandre. Though I was wet to the bone and slowed by the water that was covering the road, even at a distance I could see Abilio amid the ruins of the house. Bricks and planks, beams and tiles, sole leather and tools lay in a heap. Underneath it all, Abilio, stripped to the waist, was trying to find what was left of the old man as the seemingly endless rain came down. Paula—and this was the first time I had seen her so close—seemed oblivious to the death of her father and to the collapse of the house. Black clouds were touching the earth and almost enveloping us.

"Paula, dumfounded and frightened, did not stir. As we hurriedly removed boards, I kept looking up but couldn't distinguish her from the very tree on which she leaned. With no one else around, with no letup in the rain, we finally managed to find João Cardoso's body. His body had come to pieces, but without even a sign of blood. What was left of his crumpled face, with its white whiskers, might almost have fit in my hand—no doubt that Cardoso was a corpse. When I picked him up, moments later, I noticed how small he was, how small and light.

"As for forgetting, Alexandre, I did not nor shall I ever forget. Asleep in my arms, with the rain coming down hard upon his face and his arms hanging to the ground, João Cardoso did not hear the sound our feet made in the mud. I was in the middle, carrying the dead man. Paula was on one side, Abilio on the other. Overhead, the rain. And the rain itself stood in the way of silence. For a few months, Paula stayed with us in the cave. Abilio saw to everything and, since she no longer wanted the land where she had been born and lived with her father, he traded it for this land here. A useless, cut-over piece of ground, Alexandre, which old Januario had ceded without argument. But, with their everyday contact, what I had been expecting for a long time finally happened. Paula became Abilio's wife. Along with his wife, Abilio became owner of this piece of land.

"Forgive me, Alexandre, you who were the couple's only child —but Jeronimo cannot hide the truth. And the truth, Alexandre, brings no shame. It obliges me to say that Paula, your mother, was not like other women of the valley. Since she died when you were little more than three months old, it is only natural that you know nothing at all about her. It is only natural that you do not remember even her vaguest outline, her withered arm, her empty gaze, her impassiveness toward everything. Alexandre, your mother was insane. No one in the valley, unless it was Abilio or I, knew her intimately. João Cardoso kept her hidden in the back of his house. With Abilio, your father, her life became still more isolated. She wandered about inside like a lost soul, babbling away, her withered arm forever dangling. Frequently she mistook me for Abilio. And, in an appalling sort of letdown, she often needed her husband for the least activity. To me, she was repulsive, repulsive no doubt to whoever knew her, perhaps even to Gemar Quinto himself. But to Abilio, your father, she was strangely attractive. He built a life around her sick body and devoted his existence to her.

"Thus it was, Alexandre, that her pregnancy came about. Alexandre, forgive me, but the truth is sad. Paula's legs swelled, she became deformed, and she vomited all over, at the table, in the bed. Her hair got filthy. Her belly kept growing, and her full breasts showed through the torn dress. Barefooted and with one useless arm, she may have had her eyes open but I swear to you that Paula could not see. Abilio on one occasion said: 'Jeronimo, she doesn't know she is with child. She doesn't know anything, Jeronimo.' Day and night the vigilance went on. The fear that she would get out, also the fear that, if left alone, she might do something foolish. Had it not been for me, Alexandre—I kept going back and forth—they would have starved to death.

"But I didn't see you come into the world. I saw Paula at the beginning of her pains, her hands on her belly, with Abilio keeping her in bed almost by force. I left, in the middle of the night, at Abilio's request. When I came back, the next morning, Abilio received me with the news. You, Alexandre, had just been born. Paula was asleep."

The movement of the hoe, the awareness of walls rising, their supports set in place—the world might have been concentrated in this and in Jeronimo's voice, had it not been for my extraordinary sense of discovery. I had not known my father, Abilio, well but I had known him sufficiently to recall his face in death. Only at that moment was I getting to know my mother, Paula. "She did not know she bore me," I thought, as the hoe went back and forth, mixing the clay. Then, in a fraction of a second, several images merged, fluctuating in my inner darkness. Rosalia, and the surprise on her face. Jeronimo's monstrous compassion.

At last, with the revelation that Jeronimo had just made, I could explain certain things. I could analyze myself and situate in four beings the origin of everything: the prostitute from Ilheus, João Cardoso, Paula, and Abilio. In me, the confluence. I must have been the consequence of their destinies and nothing could have been more human than the tension of my nerves, the anguish of my blood, the impulsiveness of my heart. My great uncontrollable hatred seemed to be explained. But my house would have to stand ready, and Rosalia would have to come, in order for me to recognize my error. I would have to wait for the doors to be hung and the roofing tiles to darken in order for me to admit that my existence began and ended in myself alone. And when Jeronimo came down the ladder, the house now ready to be occupied, he said:

"Alexandre, you can bring Rosalia."

Rosalia, however, came much later. The house—a narrow sitting room and two bedrooms with packed dirt floors—would, before sheltering my wife, shelter my recollections. The future with Rosalia did not worry me in spite of everything. But the faint and hazy past, tucked away among roads leading up hill and down, was my obsession. Without Jeronimo, alone in the depths of a house that in turn faded into the darkness of night, I was exposed to a siege that knew no letup. Pell-mell, the episodes arose in disorder—arose and evolved slowly, odd fragments becoming rough tableaus, completely transparent, striking the senses like physical reality itself. Inert upon my wooden bed, my eyes closed, I would let them pass, one after the other, in a game that left me intoxicated. I could hear their voices. I saw their bodies. But the tangle of figures and settings fluctuated as if projected upon liquid, a world of the disembodied who kept their distance like shadows placed beyond life. Seeing, hearing, feeling—thus I covered the ground between Jeronimo's last report, my father's death, and my unforeseen acquaintance with Rosalia.

"Paula was asleep," came Jeronimo's voice, which was becoming locked into one rhythm. Finally, it died out. Then, since I felt it impossible to draw more words out of Jeronimo, I created in my mind the absurd period of my childhood, which I no doubt did not hesitate to accept as true. Possibly my dream has been false. Probably my imagination has deceived me. Do not question, however. Listen, I beg of you.

When Abilio, hearing the unearthly cry, ran to her, he found her with her hands still in the fire. Nearby in my cradle, I was crying. Abilio pulled her away violently—in those days she was still nursing me—and could not control his rage when he saw her charred hands, her fingers curved like Gemar Quinto's stubs. She now had two misshapen black claws. But in the throes of pain, with dry eyes and dry lips, she expressed no other reaction than that of an animal that does not know why it has been struck. She sought to raise her arms, move her fingers, walk. Overcome by pain, however, she suddenly fainted in Abilio's arms. Immediately, he laid her down on the old wooden bed.

There is no silence in the valley because there is always the wind. To Abilio, who heard it at that moment, its sound, blending with my cries, was excruciating. Without knowing exactly what to do, without even knowing to whom to turn, and knowing that only a miracle could bring Jeronimo, he raced to the kitchen. He picked up the wooden bowl full of dishes still dirty from the meal, emptied it on the brick floor and hurriedly put in it the fish oil that was used for cleaning saddles. Returning, he carefully bathed his wife's hands. Paula was barely breathing.

Then taking me in his arms—a babe of three months—Abilio waited for her to awaken. Now, however, since he had gotten used to the sound of the wind and I had become still, he could hear the crackle of the fire. In the kitchen, the burning firewood popped. Shadows of night were falling. Motionless, Paula grew vaguer and vaguer in outline as the shadows turned to darkness.

The field of Abilio's vision at last became fixed: a lighter spot at the head of a large, dark splotch.

He lacked the courage to light the little oil lamp. Next he returned me to my cradle—if I can call that cotton hammock held open by a stick, a cradle—and fell down at Paula's side, exhausted, as if she weren't there. In the middle of the night, hearing her moans, he awakened. He got up, his mind on the light, his wife, Jeronimo. Striking the horn lighter and finally lighting the little lamp, he saw Paula's face once more. Terrifying, his wife's face. Muscle spasms had set in. Her jaw seemed to have stretched and her twisted mouth forced open in a hideous kind of smile, as her eyes sparkled. Moved by a strange compassion, Abilio bent down and, though unable to repress his fears, clearly felt the sweat of the body touching his. He sought to speak but then understood it would be to no avail. Probably she was thirsty. He ran to the kitchen and when he returned with a cup of water, he observed that her legs, arms, and body were doubled in a knot. Panting, burning with fever, her muscles rigid, Paula could no longer see or hear. And when he attempted to open her mouth, to introduce the liquid, he noted that her teeth were tightly clenched. He set the cup on the floor, and his hands now free, vainly tried to force her teeth open.

Abilio did not know it, but it was tetanus. Her minutes dwindling, her contractions becoming a monstrous torture, shrieks replacing her moans—thus dawn found them. The man was helpless before the suffering of his wife, who labored to breathe. His wife slowly dying, the rigidness enveloping her, her inner world extinguished like the sooty lamp on the wall. I, a babe, sleeping. Outside, the eternal wind in the valley. Jeronimo still absent.

But it was to be Jeronimo who would prevent Abilio's witness-
ing the moment of death. The knock at the door, the loud voice
—possibly death entered with Jeronimo and with the wind
channeled through the open door. More swiftly than the men, it
reached the woman's stricken body—and when they approached
there was only the rictus that had not been relaxed.

The warmth of the earth absorbed the presence and definitive-
ly interred the image of Paula. Her child, however, kept growing. Unapproachable, once more consumed with the hatred that
had brought him to the valley, Abilio did not have for his son
the patience he had had for the mother. His black beard hid his
emaciated face. He hardly slept or ate. Cut off from others,
despising his everyday chores, running away from his home to
the most secluded parts of the valley, he converted the world
into a kind of totally empty desert. He had banished even Jeronimo. In banishing his friend, he in his indifference had offered
no objection to Jeronimo's taking me, his own son, to his cavern.

A cavern and nothing else—such was Jeronimo's home. Four
stone walls, straight up and down, inside the rock. The floor is
hardened clay with a large, flat projecting rock serving as a roof.
There are no windows. But the door, its only entryway, is a single
piece of wood hewn with an axe. His bed, an oxhide. A clay pot
and a triangle of bricks that concentrate the fire and support the
cauldron, also of clay. Outside, the harsh valley and the wind
at all hours. Jeronimo gave me lodging here—and here I lived
for many years. I did not go back to Abilio's house until the day
I finally saw him again. I did not exactly see him because, on the
bench where he lay, only his face could be clearly seen inside
the canvas in which he was wrapped. The face of a dead man,
of a man who, an hour earlier, had stumbled and fallen into the
muddy slough. He had broken both legs in the fall and perhaps

his death throes were brief in the viscid mud. He had been found dead and it was of course Jeronimo who washed his face, wrapped him in the canvas sheet, and, lifting me in his arms so that I might see him, said: "That's your father." The canvas sheet was his shroud.

After my discovery of death on my father's face, Jeronimo's cavern began to get smaller. The wind would hammer at the cracks, water would trickle down the rocks, the fire was never out. For one like myself who still lacked a sense of solitude, that which asserted itself as life was a kind of extreme freedom. Jeronimo's rough exterior, his silent presence, the wind that was as much a part of my body as my blood itself, in no sense held back the awakening of my childish curiosity. From Jeronimo I learned to milk the goats, roast meat on the spit, cook manioc. I discovered the water hole and before long was helping Jeronimo with the planting. Afterward, without even knowing how, I found the road. In its dust, far more than in the company of Jeronimo, I got to know the valley, its people, its sky, its trees. A land in mourning, the valley was. But, since men and women live in it, here too life embraces dreams and passion, selfishness and suffering. Lost and concealed with its humanity among the mountains, the valley revealed itself to me in proportion as I grew to manhood. The harvests especially moved me.

Jeronimo took no part. Cooped up on his piece of land, perhaps the most withdrawn of all the inhabitants of the Ouro, he always revealed an incapacity to live with others. I never saw him once at a neighbor's fireside. But I, still quite young but as much at home in the valley by now as I was in Jeronimo's cavern itself, did not miss a single one of its great harvests. In the fields, ears of corn were ripe. Men and women at work were indistinguishable. Children and dogs hunted cavies and rats. Their cries mingled with the voices of girls, the sound of the scythes, the noise of feet crushing the dry undergrowth. Before nightfall, and well before the distribution by the light of bonfires of the grain and the portion of cane for sugar-making, the great open fields were once more turned into naked earth. When they took their leave, transporting on pack animals or carrying on their own shoulders what had fallen to them, the men seemed to understand that the darkness and the wind destroyed these fragile, brief friendships. The families dispersed along the trails.

At first, I kept to myself. And, traversing the road all alone, I would return to Jeronimo's cavern. Afterward, specifically during one of the cane harvests, simply as a result of the contact involved in the work, and despite their ill will, I became linked with the Santanas. Felicio Santana was as strong a man as Jeronimo, and, crude and violent, rarely spoke to Rosalia, his daughter. Fearful of him, and perhaps because she had inherited his aggressive, impetuous temperament, the daughter had sought in me a refuge against her father rather than, strictly, her future companion. But Rosalia, at that time, was little more than a girl.

The rusted sky seemed to have marked her skin and given her eyes a dark cast. Her small bare feet contrasted with the long hair which she herself parted and which a bone hairpin kept from falling down in her face. Her cotton clothing, loose-fitting and without pleats, hid all the lines and contours of her body. Anywhere else, unless it were in the valley, a girl like Rosalia would be unthinkable.

When I saw her for the first time, she was running toward me, between the cornstalks. She ran easily, leaping over fallen logs, as swiftly as if she were being pursued. Heedless of her arms, which kept knocking off the spikes of corn, and not even seeing that I was blocking her way, she halted only when she saw she had run into me, her own head bruised and my lip bleeding. She looked at me calmly, without saying a word, and dashed away.

Such were the encounters of the valley children.

Rising in disorder like images that come forth when sleep is impossible, the past was becoming specifically limited to Rosalia. As in dreams, my recollections thinned, reality lost its sharp edges, logical order was notable precisely because of the absurdity of its movements. Until I met Rosalia, the world was simple, without abysses, entirely ruled by Jeronimo's presence. The cavern, the road, the harvests. But, with Rosalia, came my first resistance to Jeronimo. He got up off the ground, the muscles of his face petrified, and pointed at me with his calloused hand:

"Who is this girl?"

Jeronimo, at that time, was more than a father. He had been the one who, since my earliest consciousness, since the formation of my senses, had shaded me with his primitive soul. Associated with the eternal wind in the valley, almost one with the stone walls, that voice whose echo could make the hollows of the cave ring created my own voice. My hands would have been useless, had they not been guided and directed by his. Once my eyes were open, I saw him before I became aware of myself. He taught me to eat, to walk, to resist physical suffering with the passiveness of an animal. I was not afraid of him, had no cause to fear him, because he never beat me, never laid a hand on me. But, without him, without the sight of him, what would be left? Without his demanding:

"Who is this girl?"

I replied:

"She's Felicio Santana's daughter."

Impossible, however, for me to explain what I felt. To reveal the desire that was rising with a rigor as of thirst; to display Rosalia's image, alive within me, that was crowding out any other thoughts. It was not so much an attraction as a need similar to hunger that forced me to seek her. I wanted to hold her, dominate her, completely eliminate my irresistible wish for possession and satiety. Meeting his gaze, I hoped that he would discover in my flesh and blood the force that made the cattle procreate in the valley pastures. He, however, repeated:

"Who is this girl?"

I stood up also, and yelled:

"I need her, Jeronimo!"

Lowering his head, not wishing to stand in my way, he showed his reproof by his slow and apparently calm words:

"Take the woman, then, to Abilio's house."

"No," I replied, "I prefer to build my own house."

But, while Jeronimo was repressing his aversion, sharpening his axe to cut down trees, and offering to help me with the building, Rosalia discussed how to approach her father and how her brothers might react. Three grown men, these brothers of hers. In the valley, where friendship between families is inconceivable, these men—ungainly, rough, hard-working—were not afraid to sacrifice whatever was necessary to maintain tradition. And tradition, present in the chronicle of blood that affected everyone, gave the woman no right other than to obey her father, her brothers, her mate. Given orders, she was expected to carry them out. And not carrying them out, she could be punished.

Then at our third meeting, her nervous hands betrayed a deathly fright, and I sensed the fear that was sealing her lips and agitating her breasts. It was clear that her family had al-

ready intervened. Some minutes had to pass before she could get used to that darkness where only our eyes were becoming visible, and narrate that afternoon's episode. Her aggressiveness gradually replacing panic as she spoke, Rosalia at last burst out:
"You may have to fight to get me away from them!"
"But why?" I inquired.
She narrated the episode then. Motherless, and with no other woman in the house, she had been summoned by her father and told that her mate had already been selected, Chico Viegas, Canuto's son. She did not know him but knew Canuto, the owner of the brick factory and her father's good friend. Without daring to utter a word, but inwardly repressing her hatred for her unapproachable father, she had tried to walk out in the direction of the kitchen. With a shout Felicio had admonished:
"And I don't want you to see any more of that swamp rat, that João Cardoso's grandchild!"
Afterward he had explained, as if he really wanted to convince her, that Alexandre, whom Jeronimo had raised, did not even have a family. No doubt the boy deserved the valley's pity. Probably he was a crazy, indomitable brute like Jeronimo. Tomorrow night, let her bear in mind, Chico Viegas would come to call on her.
I knew Chico Viegas and I knew I had a night and a day ahead of me. No doubt I would find him at the brick factory, at Canuto's side, standing barefooted in the clay, the features of his face flattened, his wide-brimmed leather hat on his head. But to reach the brick factory, I would have to cut across almost in the center of the valley and walk a long way until the dry ground turned into moist, gray earth. My mind made up, aware of Rosalia's breathing, which was perfectly distinguishable from the warm wind, I promised:

"Chico Viegas will not come here."

In the valley, as Jeronimo was to say a little later, men live in eternal wariness. The wind shuts their doors, closes their windows, isolates their hearts. The leaden sky, like a stage forever draped in black, suggests the threat and brings the danger to mind. Hard and insensitive in its crustiness, inimical to any friendly gesture, the earth marks those who work it with its hardness, its insensitiveness, its roughness. As there is no other landscape, and its strip of forest is narrow and small, the valley strains men's nerves and corrupts their souls. Quoting Abilio, Jeronimo used to conclude:

"We who live here stand outside the doors of the world."

Chico Viegas, as I well knew, was a valley man. Like Jeronimo, Felicio, Gemar Quinto, he could not, when oppressed, avoid falling under the sway of his own hatred. He was, like any one of our number, capable of ripping me to pieces with his fingernails and wiping his bloody hands on the grass. But, how could he aspire to Rosalia, if he had not yet seen her? A simple agreement between Felicio and Canuto? A mere transaction that accommodated the interests of the farmer to those of the brickmaker? The answer would be given the moment I came face to face with Chico Viegas.

Before long, as soon as I had eaten my bowl of manioc mush and milk, I slipped the knife under my belt—the one I used for sticking pigs and goats—and made for the road, the long road that was, so to speak, the spine of the Ouro Valley. The blackened sky supplied the mist that covered the valley. And perhaps Jeronimo was still asleep when I left the road and took the cutoff that would shorten the distance to the brick factory. I arrived there at midday and, confronted with the flayed landscape, stopped to observe the defoliated trees, the bushes, and the low hills. At the top of a slope, the bare brick house seemed about to be sucked under by the clayey lake. From the closed door and the pigs loose in the mud, it was clear that no one was working that day. Canuto, however, came and opened the door.

He was surprised to see me. Bidding me come in, he pointed to the bench and I sat down just as Chico Viegas appeared. Heavy-set, chewing tobacco, constantly spitting at the wall, he kept looking me over, with apparent casualness, but very considerable curiosity. He was barefooted, and there was clay embedded under his nails. His bare chest, likewise smeared with clay, was broad. The muscles along his arms seemed ready to burst. Astutely, perhaps understanding the reason for my visit, Canuto said:

"You, of course, have come to talk with Chico."

Shaking my head in denial, unable to keep my gaze upon his son's flattened face, I answered precipitately:

"No, I want to talk to you about a load of tiles and bricks." And, raising my voice, firmly: "I am going to ask for a woman's hand and I need to build a house."

"A woman's hand?" the old man repeated, questioningly.

"Yes," I confirmed, "and the woman is Felicio's daughter."

In the valley, men speak less with their lips than with their eyes. Difficult and precarious, their expression is shifted to their gaze, sometimes to hands that make a fist, and only rarely is manifested through the voice. His lips tightly set, his eyes attentive, and with fists clenched, Chico Viegas turned to his father who was saying:

"But Felicio offered me his daughter for Chico."

"When?" I asked.

"About three days ago?"

Standing up, with never a thought to what might happen,

backing up to the wall, aware of the weight of the knife in my belt, I added:

"I also came to discuss the woman and I need the woman as much as I need the tiles. I know, besides, that Chico does not know Felicio's daughter.

"Let's not argue about that," Chico interjected. "If you want her, go ahead and keep her."

His words were slow, cumbersome, difficult. He preferred, evidently, not to have to talk, not to be involved in the business, and to go back to his clay. But, as his father showed surprise, he concluded:

"I've already told my father I detest Felicio Santana and prefer to die alone."

When I said good-by to Canuto, the transaction for the brick and tiles having been completed, for better or worse, I truly no longer had any doubts whether Rosalia would be my wife. Going home, sensing underfoot the harshness of the road, I was engrossed in the idea of sitting at Felicio Santana's table that night instead of Chico Viegas. What would he do, and how would his sons react? What advice would Jeronimo give if, by chance, he should come to know of my plan? But the road, in the afternoon, gathers the noises of the valley: the grazing cattle, the songless birds, the lost echoes, the buzzards struggling against the low, perpetually black clouds, the daily curse of the unremitting wind. Above all, there is the coarse creature of the valley passing silently by, his feet in a world of dust. Walking along, at the mercy of my own thoughts, I established as an expedient that I would not return to Jeronimo's cavern without first having put before Felicio Santana my claim to his daughter.

When I knocked at the door early in the evening, the light of my lantern falling on me, I was certain that Felicio Santana was not expecting me. But, upon opening the door, without showing the least surprise, he shook my hand and asked me to come in. Entering, I saw no sign of his sons in the room, but rather sacks full of corn, roots of manioc, and, stretched on the wall, a sheepskin. Felicio Santana, contrary to what I was expecting, seemed content. He showed me the bench, as Canuto had done, and said: "Sit down, my boy."

I could see, however, that he had been eating. The clay plate was now once more in his hands and, as he sat down on the bench at my side, bending over a bit, he seemed less interested in me than in the beef, black beans, and greens. Using his hand as a spoon—here in the valley almost all of us eat with our hands —he heaped up the food with his fingers, making a rounded mass that he could carry to his mouth. He tore the meat with his teeth. As soon as he had swallowed a few mouthfuls, and without my having uttered a word until then, he explained:

"Rosalia is in the back there, but the boys have not returned yet."

Hearing the annoying sound his teeth were making, seeing the voraciousness with which he was attacking his plate, and believing that I should immediately come to the point, I got to my feet and said:

"You of course know why I am here."

"Yes," he replied, "I know all right."

"And I am here," I added, "because earlier I was at Canuto's brickyard."

Suddenly getting up, putting his plate down on the bench so hard that it ended up falling on the floor, his filthy hands upraised, he was like a man besieged. In front of me, watching me as if he feared an attack, understanding perhaps that each of us was within the reach of the other's hands, he tried to ask me something. But, by a backward movement, I interrupted him. And, sensing that he would try to hit me, I lowered my arm quickly to facilitate the use of the knife, if need be. The door remained unopened and a tenuous light came from the small lamp. The sheepskin, before my bloodshot eyes, turned into a kind of cloak. I listened, however, to his question.

"And what did Canuto say?"

"Canuto didn't say anything," I replied, "but Chico Viegas turned the woman over to me."

Felicio Santana would have had to be other than a man from the valley in order not to do what he did. He bit his lip, his eyes ablaze, his arm muscles tense. Breathing heavily, almost as heavily as an animal, he shouted a filthy word and exclaimed:

"What a miserable coward he is!"

He spat, wiping his greasy hands on his pants, and also stepped back a little. In a tone of voice indicative of his anger, he stated:

"But you, Alexandre, will not get my daughter!"

"And why not?" I asked, observing all his gestures now.

His response was the unforeseen leap, and, when I saw that we were rolling on the floor, I sensed that his blow had knocked the knife out of my hand. I sought it with my eyes, my wrists pinned, almost asphyxiated by his huge body. With the first blow to my mouth and the blood now streaming down my chest, I finally understood that the brute would kill me. The second blow to my eyes, my momentary blindness, the stabbing physical pain, and, immediately afterward, my neck in the grip of his rigid hands. Gradually, though a black sponginess was enveloping my brain, I felt his fingernails entering my flesh, his blade-like fingers, and in all likelihood my screams were adding to his savage fury. Just then his scream brought me to my senses and, after the scream, his body, still warm and quivering, falling on top of mine. I pushed it away, with disgust. Then, with a tremendous effort, I opened my aching eyes:

"You!" I exclaimed.

Rosalia, distraught and grim, had the bloody knife in her hand.

That's the way it was, I swear. Lying on my wooden bed, Jeronimo having gone away as soon as the house was ready, I was with great difficulty reconstructing Rosalia's astounding arrival. A thick pall of smoke seemed to be interposed between memory and reality. I remembered, however, that I was burning up with fever when I removed from her hand the knife that was still warm with her father's blood. For the valley people, with the exception of Jeronimo, the truth became complicated. I myself distorted it, invented details, and created a version that relieved Rosalia of responsibility for the death of Felicio Santana. I was his assassin. The knife was mine, and Canuto's and Chico Viegas' depositions were most helpful.

In the valley, however, justice asks no clarification; it neither judges nor condemns. As in a wolf pack, enemies here can settle their own disputes, the stronger or the luckier going unpunished. Never forgetting, the valley may or may not show its disapproval. It shuts its eyes as windows are shut against the wind, and, in its impassiveness, imposes upon the criminal no restriction of freedom. When it takes action, it does so as a single body. And it acts only when, sensing in someone a danger or threat to the life of the group, it removes him, drives him out, or hangs him. Its justice is, then, spontaneous and not deliberative.

Savage in its imprisonment, with the sky overhead like a sinister leaden lid, the earth below unfeeling and scorched, and the eternal wind hastening like a phantom between heaven and earth, the valley does not try to interfere with the already abject and miserable destiny of anyone. It drives Gemar Quinto away because the leper, rotting and swelling, is capable of destroying it—but it tolerates those who go mad and forgives whose who steal. It knows full well that all of us are born to some kind of life and to a certain death. When terrified, it is a monster. When unafraid, it is tranquil like its muddy slough.

Meanwhile, in spite of the howl of the wind and of the distances that separate the houses, it listens and comments. With astonishment it saw my father arrive. It learned, with alarm, of my birth. It took worried note of my crime. Had it learned the truth—Rosalia's knifing her own father—it is hard to know what attitude it would have taken. For the valley, the daughter of a man is like his arm and it is unthinkable that it would not have become terrified at the knowledge that Rosalia, in order to save me, had not hesitated to let the blood of the one responsible for her life and soul.

But Rosalia—I thought to myself—was safe. Her brothers probably did not catch her in the act, and even before she took off her blood-splotched skirt she was memorizing the words I was stammering: "Alexandre killed our father." I can still see myself, by the light that was nearly gone, removing the knife from her clinched fingers. Trembling, and fearful perhaps of her brothers' return, she kept repeating my words haltingly. Grasping the handle of the knife, which seemed much too light, consumed with the urge to escape, feverish and still almost blind, I stepped on the dead man's arm. I made for the door, running, and when I felt the wind on my face, with darkness around me, my thoughts turned to Jeronimo. Filled with impassiveness, the valley remained indifferent to everything.

Rarely does it rain in the valley. But when it does, especially at night, the valley is transformed. The wind stiffens, the trees kiss the ground, and the dirt turns into mud. In terror the snakes invade the road. In the slough, the unsteady mud moves under the weight of the water. Shut up in their houses, men brace the walls with their bodies. In this starless, totally black world, we cannot see our hands before our eyes. To go out on such occasions is to go out to die. Crazed snakes bite the bared tree roots and as they struggle in the mud they become tangled like knots. To fall into the river as did my father is to be absorbed by the viscid mass. The valley at these times is awesome.

It was urgent for me to reach Jeronimo's cavern. Blind in the darkness, my hand gripping the knife, only my instinct functioning in the presence of the danger, I still don't know whether I ran or walked. Inwardly, my nerves had grown numb with fatigue, my reasoning had stopped. The violent wind seemed to rip my eyes and the rainwater stung them in truly unbearable torture. Had it not been for the road, the friendly old road that oriented me, dawn would probably have found me, like innumerable snakes and a few cattle and horses, dead in the mud. But after the silence that followed upon my fatigue and pain, I heard Jeronimo saying:

"It was a miracle you escaped, Alexandre."

I even had time to knock at the door. Jeronimo had found me at his doorstep, almost naked, my eyes like sores, my body bleeding. His moist hands had dried me. He heated water, dressed me, and, making me lie down on the oxhide, put a mug of rum up to my lips. He got wood and embers and stirred the fire into life again. Jeronimo's cavern overcame time and the valley, and it brought me back to life. I could breathe more easily, as my fever kept mounting, and I asked him to cut me some tobacco. Then, enduring the pain of opening my eyes, I saw he had my knife in his hand. And when I bit into the tobacco, my eyes once more closed, I understood that Jeronimo had already suspected the whole thing. His question was not long in coming:

"Who did you kill?"

"Felicio," I answered.

"I tell you, we come into this world to kill," he said.

That same night Jeronimo learned the whole story. In silence he heard me rehash the events, and my solitary voice reverberated as if I were saying confession. Closing my mouth, with my eyes still shut, I sensed that Jeronimo—for the first and last time in my whole life—touched my forehead with his hand. Afterward I fell asleep. And when I awoke, as if I had spent the entire night in the same spot, I saw Jeronimo. In the clay pot, water was already boiling over the flames. Meat was sputtering on the coals. But the valley, despite its usual look, appeared to me in a completely transfigured form.

Perhaps as a consequence of my physical pain, fever, injured eyes, I could observe that, despite the gusts of wind, the valley was maintaining an anguished silence. Getting to his feet, Jeronimo picked up the mug. He separated the leaves, made the tea, and, as if we were continuing the previous evening's conversation, he counseled:

"Now, Alexandre, you need to have an understanding with Rosalia's brothers."

"Today?" I asked.

"Immediately," he answered.

What Jeronimo's idea was as to the nature of man, I never knew and I think I shall never know. Similar himself to the valley, primitive like the stones in his roughness, he thought being born or dying were less important than taking a stand. If I had killed the father to get the daughter—the daughter was then mine by conquest. No one else, and especially her brothers, could take from me what I had won, hand to hand, in a duel. Behold the reasoning of the valley's creatures. The unburied cadaver unquestionably assured my victory. And the cadaver was the first thing I saw when, accompanied by Jeronimo, I walked once more into Felicio's sitting room. Hard and impassive, his sons' faces merged with the dead man's own face. With greasy food from the meal still on his lips, he was laid out on a bench, his arms dangling, his hands touching the floor.

Involuntarily, while Jeronimo conferred with the sons of the dead man, I sought Rosalia with my eyes. Before I could look around the entire room, the voice of one of the men made me look up:

"The woman is yours," he said gruffly, "and may she fry in hell!"

Jeronimo intervened, answering for me:

"First he will have to build a house."

The same man, unceasingly impassive as if he were negotiating to swap a calf, watching me without batting an eyelash, then put in:

"That's better, because she will be able to help bury her father."

Jeronimo and I went back home, without having seen Rosalia. Alongside me, Jeronimo seemed not to exist, his breathing eliminated by the wind, his shadow indistinguishable for lack of sun. Our footfalls, however, reverberated as in the depths of a mine. Buzzards wheeled above our heads, in circles, flying low. Burning like a cauldron, reacting perhaps to the rainstorm of the previous night, the valley was in a sweat. And it was once more Jeronimo who, pushing me off the road, pointed to the figure that was approaching. A misshapen thing that dragged itself

along, its hair falling over its shoulders, hatless, wrapped in a
sheet now as filthy and as full of holes as its body. It was Gemar
Quinto, the leper.

With Canuto's brick, wood from the strip of forest, and Jeronimo's help, I got the house up. A house like any other in the
valley. Once it was finished, Jeronimo reappeared later only to
bring Rosalia and her leather suitcase. Using the remnants of
the wood, I myself made the bed. I sewed the canvas sacks and,
filling them with cork bark, made the mattress. Together with
the brick, I had obtained the pail, the basin, the pots, pans and
plates, all of clay. I lost a few days in these arrangements, and,
when I went up to the cavern to ask Jeronimo to go and get
Rosalia, I brought my belongings home with me. Finally I was
going to start living.

Jeronimo and Rosalia had gotten there ahead of me. Pale and
thin, Rosalia received me joylessly, her head lowered, unapproachable in her silence. At the door, standing erect, Jeronimo
called out the moment he saw me. And when Jeronimo took his
leave, a few minutes later, when he reached the road and finally
disappeared in the flat valley, I then noticed that Rosalia, sitting
on her leather suitcase, was examining the house. Her eyes,
which seemed to flee mine, would go and come, from roof to
walls, from walls to floor. Bare and still dirty from the dust of
the road, her feet did not stir.

With the door slammed shut by the night wind that was now
blowing more violently against it, and by lantern light, I waited
for Rosalia to speak. She faced the light as she now turned toward me, wearily and as if in panic. Her face was no longer the
same. In its unchanged outline, the serenity she had shown
among the cornstalks was not to be found. In her almost infantile

expression, the wildness that was so striking at the time I saw her with the bloody knife was missing. She was like the victim of a terrible shock, the deep orbits of her eyes darkening her gaze, her breath perceptible in the movement of the air; without saying a word, she revealed the grossness of the episode that I was to learn of immediately thereafter.

My curiosity grew when, taking her by the arm, I asked her to come into the bedroom and the kitchen. We needed to open her suitcase and set things in order. We could, if she wished, look at the valley by night and hear the wind outside. When she got up, she groaned. Compressing her lips to shut out the pain, making an effort to walk, she was quite unable to hide her weakness. And thus she walked, unsteadily, to the bedroom. When her hands touched the bed, without my even having time to help her, she fell upon the mattress, crying out softly:

"I can't go on!"

Bending over her, as I struggled to control the throbbing blood in my veins, I could see that she had fainted. I went out to the sitting room and returned with the lantern, setting it on the floor. From there its light filled the area, created shadows, and permitted me to see the prostration reflected in that almost ashen face. Boiling up within my overheated flesh, driving me wild, the blood distorted my vision and isolated my hand from my brain. As if they were someone else's, I saw my own hands advance, unbutton her dress, and take it off her body with her chemise. Then her naked body, that body that had so much attracted and disturbed me, made me feel enormous pity. On her thighs and waist her wounds had already turned into sores. And I had the presentiment that those wounds had been opened by a flogging with a leather rope. Rosalia, however, came from a house in the valley.

She came from the house of her brothers. Without knowing whether or not Jeronimo had noticed anything, understanding that she could count on no one else in the world but me, I gradually began to wait for her eyes to be rekindled in that faint light. I would be able to read in her pupils the history of the last few days; hear from her lips, subsequently, its tragic confirmation. But when her lips did move, then her arms, and her face slowly turned toward me and the light, I knelt and, as my sole recourse, laid my heavy hands upon her head.

Awakened, unspeaking, without in the least noticing her nakedness, she gazed forth without any sign of human pain. Perhaps she did not see me and did not even see the lantern; did not feel my hand and did not even hear the wind. That was the moment when, dominated by the force of that empty gaze, I asked myself why we were there, in the heart of the valley, so near each other and at the same time so far apart. She moved her legs and, as if to explain my discovery, said:

"They punished me, Alexandre."

And it was after I bathed her wounds, after I made her drink the tea, after we went to the window to look at the tormented valley in its well of darkness, when we lay down, the lantern now extinguished, that Rosalia revealed to me her suffering. Weak and broken by heavy breathing, her voice sounded distant. Gently, despite everything, she managed to control my instincts and keep me supine, motionless, as if I were lying on the grass watching the buzzards circle in space. What she said, anywhere else, would be considered madness. Here it was the confession of a simple, miserable woman of the valley.

"When you came in, Alexandre, I had just given Father his plate of food. He had told me early that he wanted meat, greens, and beans. My father was very fond of beans. He was sitting down to eat when you knocked at the door and came in. He wasn't expecting you but Chico Viegas. Behind the door, with my eyes at a crack in the plaster, I couldn't believe that you had come instead of Chico Viegas. But I heard your voice, Alexandre, and then I saw you. I am my father's child and know him as well as I know myself; immediately I had a feeling that you would not get out alive. My heart pounded and my tears would no longer let me see clearly. You, above all, were like a moving shadow.

"In came the dog, which was always in the kitchen, and lay down at my feet. You never once saw it, but it was a horrible creature. Roberto, my brother, had been maiming it as if it were something not alive. First he cut off its tail and later an ear. He also put out one of its eyes. But you know how Roberto is: that's the way he amuses himself. He used to catch birds, not to blind them but to break their legs. And he breaks them with his bare hands, Roberto does. When the dog lay down I could tell it was burning with fever and the air got heavy with its stench. But I could hear that you were raising your voices in argument.

"I stooped to make the dog move. I was pushing it away, with its filthy mutilated snout turned toward me, when, from the noise, I could tell you were wrestling on the floor. I leaped over the dog, went through the doorway, and, as I drew near, saw that Father would strangle you in a matter of seconds. I saw the knife, not far from me. Without knowing exactly what I was doing, the image of the dog now having crowded out the presence of the bodies that were grappling with each other, and hearing Roberto's voice in place of your groans, I grabbed the knife and with all my strength drove it into a man's back. I had forgotten, Alexandre, that the man was my father.

"It rained a lot right afterward. Leaving me, you put into my mouth the words I said when my brothers returned: 'Alexandre killed our father.' They looked at me, with their usual hard faces, and, in my presence, lifted the body and laid it on the bench. Attracted perhaps by the blood, the dog came into the room. Slowly, and I can tell you that it was the only living thing moving at that moment, it went over to the pool of clotting blood. It lifted its snout, examining us with its single eye, and when it lowered it again, it was to drink the blood. I turned around to Roberto who, insensible, gave no sign of movement. Fernando continued chewing on a stalk of grass he had brought from the valley. Henrique, the youngest, finally broke the silence: 'The dog is drinking Father's blood,' he said. Fernando took the grass stalk out of his mouth and agreed: 'That's right, Father's blood.' But Roberto, as if grasping the reality that he had until then not seen, pulled a halter down from a nail and gave the dog three or four lashes. Whining, its snout still dripping blood, it tried to get away. Roberto blocked the doorway, continuing to brandish the strap. Motionless, and as motionless as Fathers' body, we watched Roberto's arm rise and fall until the dog was inert, perhaps beaten to death.

"With the halter still in his hand, now with his face completely flushed, he faced me. Fernando let his gaze come up to me. Looking away, I met Henrique's idiotic face. They were my brothers and I knew them well. Roberto stepped closer, Henrique also, and Fernando. I asked, then, what they wanted. 'You tell the truth, Rosalia,' replied Roberto. 'Don't make things up,' I said, as the dog was starting to whine and howl again, 'because you know well enough that it was Alexandre.' Roberto stepped back, attracted by the dog, the strap once more suspended to strike, when Fernando shouted: 'She's going to run away, Roberto!'

"To tell the truth, Alexandre, and despite my best efforts, I can't remember exactly what happened. I know that the strap Roberto was wielding, instead of hitting the dog, struck my breasts. I felt it again on my belly and on my thighs. But before falling in a faint, before everything ran together—the sheepskin, Father's body, the dog—I felt my brothers' hands on my arms. As I lay on the floor, like someone dead, their hands fluttered in the dark as if they were wings. Above me, something weighed down. And when the flesh tore, so strong was the pain that, recovering my senses, I saw Roberto's face joined with mine, his thighs compressing mine. I screamed in terror and pushed him away. His hands, nevertheless, mastered me and he stayed, gasping, his jaw against my head. What happened afterward, Alexandre, I cannot say. I can't tell you, Alexandre, because I fainted again.

"But, when I came to my senses, at the very moment it began to rain harder, Father's body was no longer in the room, nor the dog's body, nor Roberto, nor my other brothers. 'Probably,' I thought, 'they've taken Father's body to the slough and the buzzards will devour the dog.' I got up, almost naked, and cold. And it was when I started to bathe, behind the house, near the pigsty, that I saw how bloody I was. Sick at my stomach, because I knew that the blood might as easily be mine as Father's or the dog's, smelling the air heavy with the emanations of the pigs and the rain, I thought of you, Alexandre. Maybe I thought of you out of selfishness. Without a man, Alexandre, my brothers might beat me and send me away, might turn me over to the leper, Gemar Quinto."

The woman's suppliant voice was finally still and, although I could hear her heart beating in the night, I knew that our solitude was even blacker than our souls themselves. I shrank away, in order not to hurt her wounds. Resting my head on my arm, gazing into the dark as if I were expecting dawn's light, I knew that Rosalia could hear, as I did, the noises of nocturnal creatures. Screech owls, blind bats, famished snakes. Perhaps she was waiting for me to speak. Now, however, far from Jeronimo, descending for the first time into the recesses of myself, alarmed by the strange world that somehow eliminated the very presence of the woman, I had no idea what I might say. For some minutes, unable to repress the crowding images, I made a great effort. Afterward, as I once more became aware of Rosalia's body, I perceived there was in me something more than the throbbing of blood.

I know now, after so much time has passed, how terrible it is when a man stops, and ceases to act, because of self-probing. His senses are destroyed, his instincts repressed, his nerves immobilized. But, though his eyes are blind and his body sleeps, there is no lack of that luminosity that flickers like candlelight and makes the images that lodge deep inside him lugubrious. At first, bits of earth arose, unfolded, joined, and closed around me like a womb. On all sides, above and below, sweating walls. Then, as I stood up, my upraised hands tore through the clay ceiling and, when my head came through, the sky that appeared was not ash—but the bare rock of Jeronimo's cavern. The bare stone slowly moved, losing its rust color, becoming white, delicate, alive. And Rosalia once more took possession of me; took possession, now, without seduction.

"It is strange, Rosalia," I said.

"That's the way the valley is," she replied.

"The valley!" I exclaimed inwardly without opening my lips or my eyes. Becoming animated, the images grew, one by one, foreshortened, but all of them maintaining their natural proportions.

Jeronimo's cavern came first. Then, the strip of forest. The muddy slough. Canuto's brickyard. The implacable sky. The earth's desolation. Seeing it, aware of something like a grayish stain that seemed to have no structure, I almost did not recognize it. I looked in vain for the shadows of its trees, its mornings, its mute birds, but I found only the great road, the dry dust, the cracked earth, and human footprints. And the strong wind, violent in steady, hot, unceasing blasts.

Abruptly I moved my arm and my head brushed Rosalia's shoulder. She moved away a bit, on the bed, and my eyes finally opened. In the dark, her eyes shone like coals. They were two pearls that flashed restlessly and revealed their fear of a life they had not asked for. They went out, suddenly, but then surged up again quickly with more brilliance and greater anguish. The light, in one no less than the other, completely dominated the blackness and seemed to create the voice that demanded of me:

"And is there anything, Alexandre, beyond the valley?"

"Jeronimo thinks there is," I answered.

I thought, then, of Father. An outsider, my father. How he had come, what trail he had discovered, what mountains he had conquered, what inspiration he had found to orient him, I did not know. But he had come to Jeronimo's cavern, to give me soul and body, perhaps to remind the valley that the land spills over far beyond the edges of this plain maddened by wind, man's insensibility, and the heat of the sun. The valley had killed him, that was also true. Sad and pitiless, aggressive and somber, the valley had not accepted him; hands of a different sort of humanity had soiled his unearthly purity. It had killed him, strangled him, in the mud. After him, no one else entered to violate the road, to beat at the door of a stone house. Closed within itself, without doors for exit, isolated like a crag, the valley appeared to me as I had never seen it before in my life. A tomb, almost. We, its dead. We could of course exist like animals, but always beyond time, truth, and death. We could live at the lowest levels of sense impulse, victims of our primal instincts, but we were eternally ruled by consciousness of ourselves. Here, as in that world that had expelled my father, such a consciousness could not be dominated like a wild colt, but imposed itself upon us like the wind upon the valley. In my case, it might be in my brain or in my nerves, between bones and flesh, or simply in the complete paralysis of my will. I did not know this, I confess. But I felt it awaken in the night—while Rosalia was falling asleep, while my own body was plunging into exhaustion—and, when I awoke, it occurred to me that we would overcome it only through violence or in our final agony.

Though uncontrolled, the rush of my ideas had a certain logic. I realized I did not need to leave the valley. I should remain in its confines as in my own house. Look for the next morning every night, wait for the next night every morning. Now, as if they had been lost in the chill of the air or in the warmth of my blood, Rosalia's words were born again, resounded, became perceptible like objects. And Roberto occupied my whole field of vision: he had the eyes of the cadaver, the body of the dog; he was a hideous worm smothering Rosalia's mouth. Unfailingly, like a demon that never sleeps, my self-interest did not hesitate: " And what if Rosalia should have a child by Roberto? What if the sister had a child by the brother?" I got up with a bound, my mind now on Jeronimo, and lit the lantern.

Its light, at that moment, brought luck. Rosalia was sleeping and seemed not to be dreaming.

PART TWO

Do NOT ABANDON ME NOW, when I am exerting total self-control in order to test, with my own hands, the roughness of the black walls. Raised up like charred human parts, perhaps oblivious to our voices, I cannot say whether or not they perceive my presence, my breathing, the light of Jeronimo's lantern. The wind gusts whip them. Not even screech owls seek them. The very snakes, perhaps fearing a new fire, flee from the shadow of them. They are columns of ruin, witnesses to my past, all that remains of my life with Rosalia. Jeronimo's sweat, which seems to hold them up, has long ago turned into mortar. The stains have gone from my fingers. Seeking some remembrance of Rosalia, all I find is a thin layer of slime and cinders. There are not even any rats' nests. Irremovable, at rest in the night, the walls are dead in a sleeping valley. Thus, blind and deaf, they terrify me. Do not abandon me, I implore you.

Come closer, closer and closer, and do not be afraid to be involved in the enormous silence, in the throbbing air, in the mournful landscape that is projected in me as in the eyes of a dead man. Though weak, the light of the oil lantern is enough for all of us. It, rather than I, represents life. If you look carefully and come close, you can all see the overgrown bushes, the broken tiles, the skeletons of pigs and sheep that could not escape the fire. It could have been worse, I know. The house, the pigpen, the planted fields, could all have remained standing. But as a tribute to their permanence the gallows would also have remained—and, for a few days, struck by the wind, the heat, the buzzards, my body hanging from a crossbeam like a sinister pendulum.

But it's useless to go in search of anyone else, the specter of the woman or the shadow of Jeronimo, here, at this hour, at the far end of the valley. No less useless to fall back, to return to the road and knock on the door of the first house. Lost in themselves, submerged in the darkness, dazed by the wind, the valley dwellers would not hear the knocking. No one, even if I called out my name, would answer.

The valley is too alive ever to go and hide, too self-centered ever to let itself be buried in the rough, rocky ground. It would become impalpable, without body, without presence, without space. And once more you must have seen my poor human figure, barefooted in the ashes, back again among the black walls.

Come closer, then, and take pity upon this shape that is being absorbed by the nocturnal fog. His arms hang down, his mute face is uplifted in blind contemplation of a reality that is no longer real in time but lives secure in the depths of him, along with blood and tissue, like a cancer that does not kill. Still another time it will unfold—and still another time abandon its place of refuge, slowly, silently, to transfigure the desolate outer world and breathe life into cadavers. Look close and you will see that the black walls are losing their blackness, once more are merging with their mortar, to find shelter under the roof tiles. There is the bed, Rosalia's voice growing silent as her breathing becomes heavy, the room that the lantern lights. Flesh covers the skeletons of animals. And the shadow, projected by the light, obliterates the woman's face. It is my shadow. Narrow misshapen shadow that seems to want to flee, to escape at the shout from the depths of my consciousness:

"And what if the sister has a child by the brother?"

Before I could get closer, before I could stifle that anger which in the valley is the effect of solitude, I stopped in front of the woman. Her arm was drawn up at an angle, her jaw in a curve, her lips unmoving. I could see her hand, beads of sweat on her forehead, a leg that protruded from the covers and seemed to belong to another body. Without success, with great effort, I tried to make her small again and revive in Rosalia the girl from the valley. Growing up motherless, day after day putting up with Roberto, her father making her carry the baskets, making her sleep on the floor. Taking beatings from her brothers, cuffs and blows from her father—still, as I did, hearing the wind at night and in the mornings contemplating the road always spreading out like a large stain. Her smooth white belly, naked as if in defiance of the light, contrasted with her brutish feet. Though hardened and marked by the harsh road, her feet were nonetheless in harmony with her tortured face.

All I can say is that I did not touch her. She was altogether different from me, this woman. Something entirely alien, perhaps even with different bones, was this capacity to accept in the depths of her flesh the gestation of another miserable creature like Roberto. But, while Rosalia thus seemed to me to resemble a world even more painful than the valley, the specter of my mother loomed above her. Her gross and hideous body had become one with Rosalia's, and a heavy mask covered her face. Insane, unaware of her own presence, tearing her hands with her teeth in her struggle against the pain of expelling her child. And there was her child, now, seeing the phantom arise that finally permitted the return of reality: Rosalia on the bed, the lantern in my hand, its light interfering with the image of Jeronimo in my eyes.

I do not know precisely what it was, whether the image of Jeronimo or the light of the lantern, but something, other than myself, led me out, first to the sitting room, later to the yard. Awaiting me there were the stripped trees, the wind, and the dark sky. The tranquillity of the valley, thus in darkness and in sleep, without the slightest doubt unconscious and prostrate, would mislead anyone else. Not me, however. I could feel the heat escaping from the dry earth and perceive inside it, like larva in an incurable wound, human beings that were devouring one another without pity, without hope, without justice, because of fate, condemnation, and punishment. It opened up its stomach for me to see, like an insatiable mouth. Razor-sharp, its teeth cut through the mists. But the miracle of light, bringing me a fervor unknown to the valley dwellers, gave me back my eyes and hands. Above all, it gave me back my instinct.

I went back, then, into the house. I fastened the door with the wooden bar, and no sooner had I put the lantern on the floor than I was stopped still by the sight of my own feet, flat, thick, and heavy. I raised my hands and touched my hair that, cut to the middle of my forehead and covering my ears, was still full of dust. My fingers went to my mouth and I perceived my teeth, strong, hard, sharp like a saw. Finally, I opened my enormous, calloused hands, tougher than plowshares. And these hands, once more lifting the lantern high, accompanied me to the bedroom.

Rosalia was no longer asleep. Seeing me enter, she asked: "Where did you go?"

"Outside," I answered, "to look at the valley.'"

In the light, looking paler than ever, she seems not to be dead only because her eyes are gleaming. She lifts her arms, in an extreme effort, but they fall back, limp, upon her breasts. Her lips become thin, her teeth appear, and I wait in vain for the return of her voice. But the desire that tugs me, that forces me to enfold and conquer her body, is savage and free. I blow out the lantern, and when I bend down, seize her by the head, finally cup my mouth to hers, Rosalia pushes me away, quaking and horrified. I withdraw, aware now that the very darkness is burning with fever, and I hear her first request:

"No, Alexandre, please. My wounds are still open. They're infected, Alexandre, and they hurt."

The valley sun, which seems to fear the wind, withers, sears, suffocates, but its light has no brilliance. It filters down as if through a huge fog, depleting itself on the crags of mountains, on the edges of rocks, to reach the valley with a colorless flame. It is like a gas that dries the sap and weakens the roots of all vegetation. It is like a bolt from hell that provokes men to hatred,

drives them crazy, and alienates their hearts, which turn to stone
like the calcined earth. Seeing its light, on the morn whose birth
I had witnessed at Rosalia's side, I thought about all that I
must do: deepen the well, clear weeds from the yard, and cut a
tree trunk in the strip of forest that would serve as a mortar. But,
hearing Rosalia's weeping, I thought of Jeronimo. Without him,
I knew I was mutilated. I did not know how to reason clearly. I
had not been able in the least to collect my thoughts. "Could
Rosalia stay by herself?" While I feared to leave her thus in the
depths of her delirium, came the hope stronger and stronger:
"Jeronimo, why doesn't Jeronimo come?" As if seeing a mirage
on a sultry day, my eyes deformed one end of the valley, and instead of the high hazy mountains, what I saw was Rosalia in the
arms of Roberto, her brother. I turned around and, there in the
room, faced with her body's retreat, I withdrew, determined now
to go and look for Jeronimo.

Walking along, for diversion I observed my naked arms, my
feet on the hard earth, trying in vain to convince myself that
nothing would happen to Rosalia. Her fever, which was now
quite high, would keep her from awaking. And even if she did,
she could easily suppose that I would not delay. Perhaps she
would think I was in the strip of forest, cutting down the tree for
the mortar. But, although I was almost running, my instinct was
strong enough to make me leave the road when I noticed Gemar
Quinto's hut, deserted and silent. Not a bird was flying, not a leaf
moving. He was probably, at that moment, dragging himself
through the remotest parts of the valley. Thinking of him, making the impossible effort to understand his life, I became aware
of Jeronimo's presence only when I heard his voice. His fat
cheeks were unable to divert my attention from his bull neck.

"I was going to your house," he said.

"And I was going to look for you," I put in.

"Why?"

"Rosalia came to me quite sick," I replied, precipitously, "and I think she may be going to have a child by Roberto. He got her that way, Jeronimo, her brother did. Rosalia told me all about it. The others held her. I still have not touched her, Jeronimo. It was her brother, Rosalia told me so."

Jeronimo shut his eyelids tight to hide eyes suddenly bloodshot, bit his lip, rubbed his long mustaches with his fist. Standing before him, I, who knew him capable of ripping a human chest apart with his teeth to pluck out a still beating heart, observed the immobility of all his muscles. His voice, however, flowing easily, perplexed me:

"Let her not die like your mother," and, as if he were speaking to the boy in his cavern, he added, "Wait, Alexandre, wait and see if there really is a child."

"And what if the child is born?" I asked, suddenly, without thinking.

"Wait, Alexandre, wait," he repeated. "But, if the child is born, it will be necessary for you to kill it and make the father eat its flesh as buzzards eat the carcasses of calves. Wait, however, Alexandre."

He took me by my arm, which was now steady, and contemplated the valley. Trees no less sad than we, but facing upward as if they were afraid to see the spectacle of our passions and misery. After maintaining the long silence that followed upon our conversation, Jeronimo and I were on our way through the valley once more. Perhaps he was no longer thinking, no longer aware of the lusterless sun, only his organs functioning to sustain life. As for me, I breathed without noticing the dust, walked without seeing the bushes and the grass bent by the wind. I was going home. And Jeronimo, who was with me, represented support as always. Once more I felt secure and strong.

We found the door open. Stopping, Jeronimo spread his hand and washed his face with his own sweat. He pushed me aside and took the lead, while my thoughts were on Roberto. He had been there, had no doubt been spying on my movements. He had taken advantage of my absence. He had gone in. What had actually happened? The need to satisfy my curiosity was limitless, stronger perhaps than the fury of my senses. Jeronimo quieted me. Stepping aside and permitting access to the room, he let me see Rosalia, now calmer, sitting up in bed. She was not moaning or gasping. She was observing Jeronimo with naturalness—I, however, glimpsed something to come in the slight tremor of her lips. And, drawing near, I asked:

"Was someone here? Roberto was not here, was he?"

I do not know whether Jeronimo observed or not, but I saw her hands close, nervously, on the mattress. I was impressed by the decisiveness of her answer:

"Roberto was not here."

Some distance away, leaning against the door, Jeronimo said nothing. He shifted his gaze from Rosalia to me, from me to Rosalia. And he kept on chewing tobacco, his immense shoulders drooping.

"Then no one was here?" I insisted.

"Yes," she replied, "Gemar Quinto."

"Gemar Quinto!" I exclaimed.

"Yes," she confirmed, "the leper."

Jeronimo's face was what I sought for. Its tense muscles, however, were unmoving. Its eyes, immobilized. Shaggy and insensible as always, his mere presence made me walk over to the bed and take hold of Rosalia's arm. Her face looked unfleshed. Her lips, bloodless. But her voice, rising immediately, was still the same because it rang out cleanly:

"I drove him away, with my shouts, and he left. He stayed only a minute. Less than a minute, perhaps. He no longer has a face, Alexandre. Just a mass of spongy flesh."

I lowered my gaze, as soon as Rosalia had finished speaking, and I saw that Jeronimo's feet were moving, walking, heavy and splayed, his toenails worn away. When I let my wife's arm go, he took me by the arm. Rosalia had lain down again and Jeronimo said:

"Let's go clean out the shed."

Outside, while Jeronimo was at the doorway in the sunlight, I heard the neighing of the horses. They too were indomitable scions of the valley, with smooth coats, long manes, slender flanks, their ears and nostrils presaging men's violence. Even as colts, they resisted being tamed and, with no ropes to check them, were turned back to the Ouro Valley as the loveliest part of its wild landscape. Seeing them, and we saw them but rarely, I recalled the afternoon that Jeronimo, with the two Luna brothers, had caught one. As a child, I had not understood that the valley looked on this as entertainment.

For the first and only time the Luna brothers had entered the cavern where Jeronimo was sitting on the floor roasting a leg of mutton. Farther inside, I was playing with the dead ewe's lamb. I would pull it by the tail, and with no knife in my hand, try to imitate Jeronimo slitting its throat. Bursting in amid loud guffaws, the Luna brothers probably did not themselves know why they were there. No doubt they were roaming the valley, with nothing in mind, and came on Jeronimo's cavern as they might have any other. The door was open, so they went in. I saw them, and though I didn't see them very much afterward, I was never to forget them.

You would have called them twins, they were so alike. What distinguished one from the other was not the rags they were wearing, nor their hairy chests, bushy eyebrows, black curly beards, tiny eyes almost out of sight within puffy sockets, but the scar showing on the neck of the one who seemed to be the older. "Maggots got in a sore," he had explained. With their leather hats in hand, they came up to Jeronimo, exchanged a few words, and left. I followed close behind bringing the dead ewe's lamb.

On the door outside, the still bloody sheepskin, stretched by Jeronimo, caught their attention. One of the Luna brothers exclaimed: "That would make a nice saddle blanket!" At that very moment we caught sight of the horses cresting the hill, trampling the underbrush. We heard their strong aggressive neighs. In no time a plan had been devised to catch one of the horses. Jeronimo went back to his cave and got a rope that he himself had plaited. He headed for them, stooping low among the bushes, then, setting his feet, he threw the leather rope from afar with his huge arms. It sailed through the air, as swift as an arrow, its great loop open, but before the Lunas could run forward, I saw the wild stampede of the herd. Jeronimo gave a shout and his voice surmounted the noise: "Come, quick!" Not far away, with the Lunas closing in, I could see that Jeronimo, his legs set wide, was having trouble holding the snorting animal. His arms, erect, seemed the prolongation of the leather rope itself.

Given no letup, now bucking now running, the animal let the distance grow less and less. Rearing, its hooves dancing in space, it would have attacked Jeronimo, who kept shouting, if one of

the Lunas had not grabbed for its ear. When it lowered and shook its head, still kicking, its flanks quivering, he managed to jump on.

But the other Luna immediately went for its mane, bellowing like a madman, and Jeronimo could then slip the rope around its legs. The animal tottered and finally fell down in a cloud of dust. Sweat ran hot down its neck and flanks.

Though pinned, it could still move its head. At that moment, sweating as much as the animal, one of the Lunas beat out its eyes—its clear, beautiful eyes that soon turned into a bloody pulp. The animal quivered, snorted. Finally, while Jeronimo was spitting on his hands, I saw the two Lunas start a rip with a piece of stick in the horse's mouth. Once they had made the cut, amid spurting blood, on the still struggling body, they used their own hands, their fingers gripping its teeth, to complete the tear that transformed its mouth into a gaping horror. Then they sat down on top of the animal, both gory, and started guffawing again.

Jeronimo turned his back on them and returned to the cavern carrying me in his arms. With my eyes shut, sprawled in Jeronimo's arms, I could still see the horse dying.

He began to stir, again chewing his tobacco, as the horses moved away. It was hard to say what he was thinking; impossible, at that moment, to interrupt his silence. But Jeronimo turned around, looked at me, and said:

"She must not be left alone. Her brother Roberto may come. And Gemar Quinto may return."

He concluded, unhurried:

"You will have to stay at home like Abilio, your father."

He divided the days, then, in two ways. Some nights, he would sleep at my house; some he would sleep at his cavern. He would go and come, cutting across the valley, bringing me sometimes a quarter of beef, sometimes a jug of milk. He taught me, in that period, to cure leather, to make bridles and saddlebags like my grandfather João Cardoso. On many an afternoon, when the shed was ready and there was no work, he would return to his extraordinary topic—Abilio, my father. He would reproduce for me his nighttime conversations, around the fire, while the clay pot was steaming. " 'Not far from the valley,' Abilio used to say, 'there is an enormous world of forests.' "

"The cacao forest," Jeronimo would repeat, moving his bull neck. "You climb the mountain, cross the rocky stretch, and you come to the rain forest. It isn't actually a swamp, but the ground is wet, boggy, and cattle there don't do well because of the botfly. The horses cannot stand the mud on the roads or the diseases that come from the waters. And men live in clay houses in the remote forests as if interred among the cacao trees. Also, despite great distances, one finds ranches." And Jeronimo became eloquent: "Their villages are built less as a gathering place and more as a shelter for those who return, exhausted and defeated, from the great forests. Houses joined each to the other, Abilio used to say, and men always within earshot of their neighbors. Abilio knew all that, inside and out.

"How he got through the cacao forests," Jeronimo went on, "how he scaled the mountains, how he crossed the razor-sharp rocks, I do not know. Nor do I know how he found the valley. I still do not know what kind of sorrow deranged his life. What I do know, Alexandre, is that Abilio always ran away from himself, and he was still running away when he tied himself to a woman like Paula. The valley drew him; he probably came to the valley as others did. This is a desert here, Alexandre, and the desert always recruits those who flee."

But Jeronimo interrupted himself, frequently, now to spit out the wadded tobacco, now to watch a flight of buzzards, or again to listen for Rosalia's call. But above all, perhaps because he preferred not to talk. I, however, would insist and exclaim, with the greatest expectation:

"It is strange that he managed to live at all!"

"And live in the depths of delirium without hope," Jeronimo went on speaking, his language naturally less polished and his turn of phrase poorer. "He was as amazing in his abyss as this valley is in its own world. Abilio, I can tell you now, never occupied his body entirely. Inside him, there was room for another. It was a good thing, Alexandre, a very good thing indeed, that death carried him off. One thing, however, we never shall know."

"Never shall know?" I repeated.

"Yes, Alexandre. No one, in this valley, ever found out who he was. No one, Alexandre, not even I, could learn from what and why he suffered."

Finally, breaking in upon Jeronimo's great subject, the strange subject that excited us and made us forget Roberto, even Gemar Quinto, came Rosalia, who left her room and sat down beside me, in the tile-covered shed. Four months, almost. The leper had appeared once but, seeing me, had fled in his sheet, buffeted by dust and wind. The herd of horses had whinnied a few nights, in the distance, perhaps in the strip of forest. The pigs, the cactus, the hair on my face, all had grown. And Rosalia, now sitting between Jeronimo and me, could not hide what we had known for a long time: in her belly her brother's child was growing. Seeing her now cured of all her wounds, and before Jeronimo could get up, I unconsciously thought of Gemar Quinto. And, to avoid the curiosity of our eyes, the silence of our lips, I asked:

"Gemar Quinto, Jeronimo, was he born in the valley?"

"I didn't see him born," said Jeronimo, his face now as inscrutable as the valley itself. "But I would see him, even in
Abilio's lifetime, heading toward the mountain with his dogs. His
little farm was down below, there, on the short cut that leads to
Canuto's brickyard. He had a farm, Gemar Quinto, but he did
not work the land. He hated cattle, despised horses, knew nothing of planting, but loved his dogs. A hunter, Gemar Quinto. His
weakness was the night, his traps, the brushland. Solitary, and
for that very reason wary, Gemar Quinto. I awoke, innumerable
times, to the barking of his dog pack. What he hunted, I never
found out. Deer, perhaps, because their antlers decorated the
walls of his cabin. Deer or wild goats that roamed the mountain.
A hunter, Gemar Quinto."

When Jeronimo paused this way to reveal valley episodes or
throw light upon the life of one of its inhabitants, whether João
Cardoso, Abilio, or Gemar Quinto, the impressive thing was the
vigilance of his eyes. He seemed not to remember but to see. He
felt as if he were experiencing everything he said. And he com-
municated to us, to Rosalia and me, the tension or the terror of
events, his voice setting our nerves on edge. He would animate
reality and then cut it into pieces with the same patience he
showed when he cut up a steer or mended a saddle.

"A hunter, Gemar Quinto. They used to say he handled a bow
like an Indian, and in him truly there was much of the redskin.
With his smooth face and straight hair, ever alert, suspicious
and resistant, he could jump over barriers, roast a goat, raise
game better than anyone. Possibly his parents had stayed on
here, in the valley, when the redskins fled. As prickly as a porcu-
pine, speaking little, this half-Indian lived more in the recesses of the mountain like a goat than actually in the valley.
Now and then, always with his dogs, he would appear at João

Cardoso's shop to trade some of his game. Gemar Quinto, a hunter.

"When the disease started, I no longer recall. Abilio was still alive, and it was he who warned me that Gemar Quinto's rash was leprosy. Where he had gotten it, I don't know. As there are always drought refugees getting lost in the mountains, it is hard to be sure, very hard, Alexandre. Someone he had met had transmitted the disease. His first victims, however, would be his dogs."

Jeronimo stopped, perhaps without noticing Rosalia, who was resting her hand on my leg. Once more his face became inscrutable. In the rigid muscles that helped compose his vigilant, sharp-focused gaze, I saw the loathsome image of a man running. Under his gaze, Gemar Quinto was already a fugitive. Insulting arms were driving him away. But his eyes closed, and his voice came back harshly, as if warmed in the valley's light.

"Gemar Quinto's leprous dogs will not soon be forgotten in the valley. Stoned to death, from a distance, at their master's door. The burning of his house, his escape out the door, bursting through the smoke. The forest gave him refuge and everyone was alerted, forewarned, worried. Abilio died, so did João Cardoso, but the leprosy keeps Gemar Quinto alive. To hear people tell it, he is a mass of decay. His whole body an open sore. He doesn't speak for he has no tongue. But he walks, stumbling along, as invincible as the valley."

It was night, finally, when Jeronimo went to bed. I shut the door, flipped the wooden latch, Abilio and Gemar Quinto occupying my thoughts; my annoyance was greater in the presence of Rosalia who, sitting on the bed, seemed to be waiting for me. She stood up, when I approached. She was less a woman, at that instant, than a being with no fear, something as quiet and unfeeling as a door. She did not laugh, did not look about, for a few seconds did not make a single movement. Her disheveled hair fell down over her shoulders and protected her breasts. When her voice cut the night's silence, although my nervous tension had diminished, I confess I shuddered. She, however, repeated the words:

"He is worse than the leper."

"Who?" I asked.

"The child,'" was her reply.

Jeronimo was nearby, separated from me by a door. "Roberto's child," she understood. "The child worse than the leper," she had said. At that moment I had an urge to burst out: "It's your child," but the image of the struggling horse invaded my vision and I felt on my hands the warm blood of the animal. In her face, which seemed coarser in the light, what was reflected was not nausea. Merely the energy of one who cannot forgive herself her own human condition, the hatred of one who is resolved to oppose injustice. Without moving, she added:

"Can I not tear it out of me?"

The door, Jeronimo just beyond it. Should I open the door and call, Jeronimo would appear. "The child worse than the leper," she had said. Roberto beating the dog. Gemar Quinto no longer has a tongue. The tobacco Jeronimo chews. "The child," her answer. I cried out, confused by the play of images, the valley's heat drying up the saliva on my teeth:

"No, woman!"

She stopped, her hand upraised, the mute word on her lips, her eyes on the door. "On the other side, Jeronimo," she was perhaps thinking. And, turning her back on me, she got in bed. She wept not at all. She showed agitation not in the slightest. Once, during the brief moment I remained standing, she extended her arm, cupped her hand, felt her belly. "She's thinking of the child," I reflected. But something made her get up and, coming so close I could feel her breath, she asked:

"Then that's why you don't want me?"

"Roberto's child," I said, as if Jeronimo were speaking for me, "as long as there is your brother's child, Rosalia, you cannot be my wife."

"And when the child is born?"

Before I could answer she exclaimed:

"I will kill it as soon as it is born, I swear by the body of my father."

"No, you will not do that!"

I held back, restless, in the hope that she would speak no more, and, as if reading the request in my eyes, Rosalia returned to the bed and lay down, indifferent to the valley that covered us like a blanket of iron. Jeronimo was asleep, beyond the door. But I, sad animal indeed, incapable of knowing then that nature is no respecter of man, man's sorrows, man's laws, could not imagine that Rosalia was stronger than the valley. Wide awake, breathing perceptibly, she seemed to have prearranged the silence so that we might, as always, hear the bats struggling with the wind. Gemar Quinto had probably already shut the window of his cabin. Jeronimo, just beyond the door. When my hands finally opened, heavy as valley earth, and covered my face, I was not aware of the dark. I wished, however, that my heart would stop beating. And that some other world would replace the inert valley, its landscape now as motionless as my own blood.

In the early morning, when I set out with Jeronimo to accompany him to his cavern, Rosalia was still asleep. I had already annnounced that we would leave early, with a lantern to guide us for a while, and that I would return, without Jeronimo, before evening fell over the valley. We walked the wet road without exchanging a word. Like a shadow, I was accompanying Jeronimo with nothing on my mind. We met one of the Luna brothers, the older, near Gemar Quinto's cabin. He pointed to the leper's house and, out of sunken eyes, informed us:

"He hasn't come out for two days. I don't think he'll escape."

Jeronimo, however, seemed totally unconcerned. He continued walking, as did I, in silence. The leper was no longer able to walk, the older of the two Lunas had informed us. But he soon took his leave and, according to him, was going to visit Canuto at the brickyard. In silence, we went on. Invariably the same, the Ouro Valley. Violent and sad, its wind. Its ground, a rocky shell. The muddy slough, fetid and putrescent. Jeronimo, its child. It explained Rosalia's pregnancy, the wild horses, the savage energy, the jagged rocks that ripped the mountain tops. It would also explain, shortly, the death of Gemar Quinto.

Jeronimo pushed open the door to his cavern and we went in to see what I had always seen, since childhood. Then I helped him clear ground for his new manioc crop, repair a part of his pigpen, castrate a goat. Since we finished earlier than planned, and even today I really don't know why, I suggested:

"You could go back with me, Jeronimo."

He did not hesitate. He washed in the wooden tub, sharpened his knife on the very stone that formed the wall of his cavern, and, side by side always, we walked back. It was still day, in the valley. The unfailing wind, which seemed to be increasing in force, blew against our bodies. No buzzards in the sky. Rare the men and women on the road, invariably silent, as if fatigued, almost aggressive. But when we reached the strip of forest, with

Gemar Quinto's house nearby, we sensed that night would not delay. We hurried on. And we could see my house by the last light of the sun.

Rosalia was not waiting for us. Jeronimo halted, his lantern in hand. I went forward and, with my fingers, rapped on the door. Distinctly came the murmur of the wind in the trees and bushes, the noise of the pigs, but, from within, not the slightest sound. I rapped again, nervously, Jeronimo closer to me. Nor was there, even this time, any sound. Then I called out to Rosalia. Next I shouted her name. When we understood that she was not answering—darkness was invading everything and blinding the valley—Jeronimo put the extinguished lantern down on the ground, took a firm grip on the door, pushed it with all his might. It creaked and shook, but resisted. Continuing in silence, he challenged its resistance with his shoulder. His muscles bulged. Finally, his entire brute force having been concentrated on it, the door swung open and Jeronimo almost fell over it into the house.

We no longer could hear the noise of the pigs, nor the sound of the wind in the trees. Darkness, moreover, did not allow us to see a thing. Jeronimo commanded:

"Light the lantern!"

With difficulty, I located the lantern. I grasped it and when I lit it, in the sitting room, I saw Jeronimo's arm, elevated, pointing upward. I raised my eyes quickly, with a strange energy fortifying my nerves, and only then did Rosalia appear to me. Her motionless feet. Her body, stiff. Turned upward, with its dying spasm still imprinted, her face was partly hidden by the hair that had fallen over it. The leather halter, which held her body up by the neck, was fastened, overhead, to the rafter. Nearly black, her inert tongue was visible. On the floor, the ladder.

Jeronimo, as always, impassive. Impassive and inhuman like the valley itself. But I felt my heart beat as never before and as never again in my life.

At first, as if Rosalia had absolute mastery over me, despite the blasts of wind that were filling the doorway, I could not move my eyelids. My eyes watched her, against my judgment, against my will. The light was tenuous, however, and the distance that separated me from that face now lost in shadows was vaster than the valley itself. Jeronimo, who had already snatched the lantern from my hands, raised the ladder, steadied it against the rafter, and went up. Betweeen the light and the shadows, almost indistinguishable to my straining eyes, his hands were working. They kept moving, one clasping Rosalia's waist, the other trying to slip the loop from her neck. Finally, Jeronimo's voice roused me:

"Come up, I want your knife."

The knife was the same one that had been in Rosalia's hands, its handle of wood, its blade well sharpened. It served me as scissors, plane, and weapon. I pulled it out of its sheath and, once more in control of myself, I climbed the ladder to hand it to Jeronimo. When I handed it to him, his mouth at that moment full of chewing tobacco, I sensed that Rosalia's body was hanging on mine. Jeronimo withdrew his arm from her waist and asked me to hold her. He would go up and cut the halter, he said, and he added:

"You will have to support her body."

On the floor, the lighted lantern. At the door that we had forgotten to close, the wind. Outside, the valley. And the knife in Jeronimo's hand. I was carefully following the knife, but, when Jeronimo cut the thong, it was all so fast that Rosalia dropped, her arms hitting my face as if they were alive, and fell like a weight. If Jeronimo hadn't managed to cling to the end of the thong, steadying the ladder, we would have fallen with Rosalia. Hurriedly, I got down. Jeronimo also. Neither of us looking at the other, we could see that Rosalia's face was bloodied.

I expected Jeronimo to pick her up—but he turned around and, lantern in hand, closed the door against the wind. He came back, approaching slowly, holding the lantern aloft so that its light might show us the woman. Her eyes were closed, her teeth seemed to be biting her tongue, there was a black splotch on her neck. And, as if it were attached to her face but at the same time removed from it, a strange expression of absence, devoid of suffering and remorse, but also devoid of peace and tranquillity.

It was as if death had not caught up with the dead.

Possibly Jeronimo was right, possibly Rosalia had felt merely a faraway presence of death. Her eyes had been suddenly blinded, her heart had stopped as if held by a powerful claw. Her head had dropped, her hair over her face, her consciousness slowing to a halt along with her organs and her blood. And after that, the blackness. In the depths of this blackness, the formation of the child ending also in death, for lack of food. But Rosalia, now beyond death, had, despite her silence that would be eternal, kept her last request for me. Her final thought, the extreme gasp of her voice, could be read in her open hands, her curving fingers, concretely expressed in the words: "I killed myself to stop the pain." Jeronimo, however, interrupted with his own the voice I was hearing:

"Now the world is too small to hold both you and Roberto."

"I know it," I replied.

But, as if nothing remained to be said, as if it were embarrassing to add a single detail, he pointed to Rosalia's body and inquired:

"And where do you intend to bury it?"

"Right here."

"Here, in the bedroom?"

"Yes, in the bedroom.'"

Turning away from me, Jeronimo picked up the lantern. He went to the kitchen, put in oil, and returning, brought the shovel and the hoe. He asked me to cover up Rosalia's body, with just anything, even a floor mat. He had already started digging when, bending down, I contemplated the dead woman's face. At that moment, merely my curiosity to look. Afterward, with the hoe striking the ground like a hammer, I understood that, even though buried, that body would accompany me. I would accompany it, also, in its putrefaction. Then I got up and, with the shovel, helped Jeronimo to dig the grave. Reddish and dry, the earth was truly the earth of the valley.

She had been born in the valley, had never left the valley, and in the valley would remain forever. The lantern light was not flickering, the wind was not chastising the walls, the valley was unaware of what was happening. Even if it knew, even if it saw us lift the body and lay it in the bed of earth, not the slightest interest would it show. For the valley, a dead person is less than a tree, even less than a stone. And Jeronimo reflected that insensibility in his tranquil look, in the movements of his hands, in his teeth that continued to chew the cake of tobacco. The moment for covering up the body having arrived, he rested his arm on the hoe handle and asked:

"Are you going to continue living here?"

I did not reply, and, if I did not, it was because I became

aware of the mean look in my own eyes projecting above his voice. My eyes kept to the narrow space. The bed, the suitcase, Jeronimo, the piled dirt. The grave, an enormous mouth. In its pit, like a child in a womb, Rosalia's body, her feet now covered, her arms upon her breasts, her face awaiting the abrupt movement of my hands that would rake in the dirt. A powerful fatigue, at that moment, overcame me. My fingers grew heavy, my eyelids drooped. Thus it was that, without any emotion and without any ratiocination, I buried the shovel in the dirt and threw some, forthwith, on Rosalia. I opened my eyes wide. Jeronimo was speaking:

"It would be a good idea also to bury the woman's things."

My empty brain suddenly let itself be penetrated by an image that was rapid, but so powerful that it set my nerves on edge and once more stirred my blood. I clutched the end of the shovel with my hands, looked straight at Jeronimo, articulated my words firmly:

"No, it's possible I may still need them."

"All right," said Jeronimo.

But I could no longer rest, by then. One shovelful after another, in front of the unmoving Jeronimo, I filled the grave. To level the floor, after tamping it, I trampled it with my feet. Hard, as before. As before, the same even floor. Jeronimo called me and we left the room. He halted, in the sitting room. He showed me the blood spots, suggesting:

"Shall I take out these blood spots with the hoe?"

"It's not necessary," I replied.

But, whether because I felt the need to walk, or because I guessed Jeronimo's thought—"No use staying here, Alexandre"— I proposed that we return to the cavern. Deep inside me, what I wanted was to breathe the air of the valley, welcome on my face the buffeting of the wind, submerge in darkness in order to develop the image that was wavering in my still confused brain. And the contrast, when Jeronimo opened the door, was tremendous. Silence splintered against the scourged trees, the nocturnal air crashed against my warm body. Dazed by the lantern light, sweeping low, bats were squeaking. Nonexistent, as always, the heavens. Only Jeronimo, who looked larger, framed against the deserted valley. At that moment, without suffering, without seeing or hearing, I had a presentiment that Rosalia's request was greater than my powers. For me, who had felt only pity for her body, she had died a virgin. Perhaps she had discovered milk in her breasts, perhaps the movements of the child in her womb, unceasing and violent, had put the gallows noose over the rafter. Ill defined, terribly vague, her torture. Her tension had been transmitted to me. Her paralyzed organs were an extension of my own. Her death became fused in me.

In my eyes, which did not see the valley, the image that had already formed would not be dissolved for a long while. It was like a cloud fed by the cauldrons of hell, day after day, evolving like a nightmare, but exacting, demanding, finally imposing complete abandon. In Jeronimo's cavern, inside my own house with her grave under foot, in the sunshine or stretched out on the bank of the muddy slough, I would, like it or not, see the shadows stripping Rosalia's bones. If it rained, I would follow the water seeping into the earth until it reached her face, her thighs, her feet. I saw vile denizens of the earth sucking her tongue, slipping like lizards across her rotting belly. I heard, hollow and short, the bursting of first one organ then another. In my nostrils the stench of rotting flesh. Her slow putrefaction, which the dense earth could not hide, seemed to me invincible, obstinate, monstrous. Useless to cover my eyes with my hands. Useless to implore the wind to make me deaf.

The clothes on my body became foul and my own body became alien to me. My hair grew, reached my shoulders, merged with my beard. My feet kept walking, often a mass of sores, but did not know what they walked upon. Hunger and thirst, solely. Vaguely, as distant as I myself, the presence of Jeronimo. Descending, ever descending, I lost contact with the wind, with men, with the valley. But it was to be Jeronimo who, some time later, would bring me the remembrance of what I had been. Without panic, I heard what he told me:

"A man dies while alive, Alexandre," he said, his voice firm, as he was helping me to escape, almost outside the valley, "and you, Alexandre, were dead. You did not want me to clean up the blood spots. You actually asked that we go back to the cavern. I had the lantern in my hand and I opened the door but, not hearing me, you kept on walking, blind, insensible, uncontrollable. I ran and, when I caught up with you, I saw immediately that you would not recognize me.

"In this valley I've seen many things. I saw João Cardoso, dead. I saw Abilio, your father. Paula, your mother. Rosalia, your wife. The like of your face, however, I had never seen in my life. You seemed to be terrified but, at the same time, you did not seem to be human. Your eyes were like an animal's. Sharp, pointed, like claws, your fingernails. Your teeth, which shone in the light, were those of a mad dog. Strange, as if strangled, your voice. That, Alexandre, is how it all began. If you slept, when we reached home, I don't know—I was rather tired and lay down and fell asleep.

"The following morning, however, I couldn't find you. I didn't see you, actually, for almost a week. I knocked at many doors, in the valley. I went to Canuto's brickyard, stopped to examine the slough, went back to your house. The men shook their heads, the women weren't talking, and the children ran. I was at the Lunas' cabin and, for the first time, I told what had happened. Rosalia, hanged. You, gone. A day or two later, Alexandre, the whole valley was giving me strange looks. Perhaps it was thinking about Gemar Quinto, shut up in his cabin, unable to walk, suffering hunger and watching death approach. Mainly, however, the valley's curiosity was concentrated upon us. It was beginning to believe, by then, that it had been you who hanged the woman.

"When I discovered you, Alexandre, you were alive—but dead. A man dead in the midst of life, Alexandre. Sprawling, with a lusterless look in your eyes. What I saw, I can't explain. Nor can I explain what I felt. As for speaking, you said not a word. And it was not without difficulty that I brought you to the cavern. You were burning up with fever, Alexandre. I washed your body, got the hot tea into your mouth, and watched over your sleep. You, Alexandre, when you awakened, were changed. You asked for my knife, roasted the meat, ate as in the old days. A pleasure to see you get your teeth into the meat.

"Meanwhile, something in you had been transformed. You were preoccupied, distant, and only your hands moved. If I questioned you, you didn't answer. You gazed at me, forgetfully, when I would call to you. I didn't know what to think, and I was far from believing that your wife's death had affected your nerves. Perhaps it was the remembrance of Rosalia, and the torment of your hatred, the frenzy of your blood throttling you. A dead man you were, Alexandre.

"At the far end of the valley, Gemar Quinto was on his death-bed. Rosalia, buried in the floor of her own bedroom. The valley, however, preferred to forget the leper and to remember the woman. To remember the woman, Alexandre, to see in Abilio's son the assassin of Rosalia's father. For the valley, you killed the father and the daughter. And that meant that the valley was beginning to see in you, Alexandre, a threat. Should you kill someone and show the knife, it would respect you. Should you hang someone and show the rope, it would not be concerned. Should you walk the road with bloody hands, it would remain indifferent. But you, Alexandre, went out like the leper, crawling, cowering, overcome by hunger and thirst. For the valley, you came back a sick man, a sick man and a killer, and that was a threat.

"But only I knew that you were dead. The master's eye, you are well aware, fatteneth the horse. And it was because I knew your state that I felt justified in going against your deepest urges of mind and body, to bring you here again into the warmth of the valley. You needed to become strong like an animal, aggressive like a snake that has been hurt, to survive. The valley will run away from a leper. But the valley will stone to death a man sick with your sickness. This is why, Alexandre, I dragged you out of the cavern that afternoon."

I still have the scars. I still remember the inner revulsion caused by Jeronimo's brutishness. He dragged me out of my nook in the cavern as if I were a dead weight, my muscles benumbed, seized by an overwhelming sense of insecurity. Outside, almost in the same place the Luna brothers had killed the horse—the valley sun did not resemble a midday sun—he picked me up by the hair. Naked from the waist up, he had no way to hold me firmly except by the hair. And, while his left hand held me, with his free hand he repeatedly slapped me hard in the face. I don't know if his savage face reflected pity or not, but I do know he was cursing. Cuffing me and cursing me. At one moment, feeling the blood in my mouth and eyes, my chest pommeled by his fists, I could distinguish the exclamation that his saliva had made thick:

"The valley, Alexandre!"

Still confused but with a mounting awareness, my senses now fighting back, I could taste the blood in my mouth. It was acid, bitterer than acid. And while my nerves were being restored, amid Jeronimo's continual beating, the outer darkness, dense at first, kept getting softer: first a cloud, then a faint whiteness, after that a few colors, and, finally, the trees, the bushes, the earth. Framed by my body, which had again reached equilibrium, my wide-open eyes—and in the circle of their vision, the sweaty jaw, the long mustaches, the flattened nose, the face of Jeronimo. Seeing me awaken, perceiving perhaps that instincts and will were merging, he cradled me against his chest and, with his hand, cleansed my face of the streaming blood.

He took me, then, to the cavern. He sat me down, my back against the cold rock and, picking up a bowl full of water, he emptied its contents over my head. I shuddered, immediately seeing better and hearing perfectly, able to ask and answer questions. The tree was once more drawing sap from its roots— but Jeronimo, not without a kind of pride, did not allow my memory to revive by itself. Jolting it, my own thoughts having retreated in space as far as the bedroom floor where Rosalia's body was decomposing, Jeronimo asked:

"What do you plan to do, now?"

My brain was working by itself. A bit beclouded, its reasoning powers slightly repressed, it elaborated its response with a rapidity that Jeronimo had perhaps not expected. The images, however, preceded my voice. And it rang out after Roberto's presence became powerful, with the whimpering dog, Rosalia curled up on the ground, and Jeronimo himself chewing tobacco. In less than a second they faded and, then, I replied:

"What Rosalia asked."

"And did she ask for something?"

"Yes, she was already dead, but she asked."

Jeronimo shook his head, and his hair, as always happened, danced over his shoulders. He said, once more impassive and tranquil:

"I understand, Alexandre," and he added, "but the valley must know!"

"Must know?" I repeated, almost shouting.

"Must know," he replied, "that only now are you going to kill. If you don't explain, long beforehand, what will everybody think? Alexandre," he concluded, lowering his voice, "I have already seen one man hanged here."

The urgent necessity in me was bigger than I was. I lacked the clear understanding that I now have, but what impelled me, my face still bleeding and my hair damp, was less the rage of a famished beast than the need to respond to the poison that was feeding my heart. Set in the earth like a huge rock, Jeronimo's image no longer interfered. Without food, without water, without a human voice to reach my ears, I would still resist everything that came my way. If they cut off my feet I would crawl, guiding my body with fingernails as hard as claws. If they burned out my eyes, tore off my arms, cut up my heart, even so I would advance with some shred of my body, hugging the earth, until I satisfied my need. I clenched my fists, looking Jeronimo in the eye, and exclaimed:

"The valley be damned!"

Jeronimo came closer, his cavern filling up with smoke from the firewood, and as he always did on such occasions, exclaimed: "The powers of fortune go with you."

I halted, however, my body bathed in sweat, at the entrance to the strip of forest. Earlier, I had met a valley man running in the direction of Jeronimo's cavern who, as he passed me, had looked away. He was running as if in great haste. I had no time to reflect because, athwart my path, men were converging in a small crowd. In the distance, the cabin of Gemar Quinto, the leper. Beneath the dark clouds, flying in circles, the buzzards seemed to scent, as we did, the pestiferous air, the wind blasts scattering the stench of carrion. I recalled the older of the Lunas, his sunken eyes, his voice: "I don't think he will escape." My surprise having passed, I understood that they feared the leper in death. Their panic was real—the wind, the eternal and inexorable wind might spread the disease, turn the whole valley into a single open sore.

The clouds rolled, as black as ever. Perhaps because I came from Jeronimo's cavern, and was driven by an obsession that had placed me beyond this world, I for a moment facing Gemar Quinto's cabin, mistook men for trees. More immobile than trees, the men were not speaking and in their silence were keeping their eyes on the sky. Now and then, a buzzard or two would bore through the low, low cloud. Their movements, however, were kept in view, and, while eyes were following their flight, everyone was perhaps imagining the leper's death throes.

He had foreseen his death, no doubt about it. Dragging himself, at the end of his strength, he had still managed to close the window, shut the door, lock himself inside in his anxiety lest his vile and decaying flesh serve as food for the hungry buzzards of the valley. Exhausted, he had perhaps fallen on the floor, still alive but unable to weep and suffer the ignominy of his pustules. Faint, the beat of his heart. Soft, the light that remained in his eyes like a challenge to the pain and to his miserable condition. As an infinite consolation, perhaps he took a final pleasure in thinking that he would not have his body ripped by the beaks of vultures. His cabin would not be violated.

But the buzzards were already alighting on the roof. They looked in vain for a crack and in vain pecked at the hard tiles. The smell coming from inside must have been strong. The dead man alone could not hear them. The noise of their beaks and their wings, carried by the wind, reached the men. They listened, in apprehension. And from among them, as if he reflected the valley's opinion, someone said:

"We have to put an end to this!"

An old man, without lowering his gaze, asked:

"How?"'

It was another man who answered, his voice rising:

"By opening the door so the buzzards can get in."

Then he added, in explanation:

"As soon as they are in, we will close the door so they can't get out."

And he concluded, crying out:

"But we need to move fast."

Move fast, indeed, because the clouds were getting darker, the wind stronger, the night in a hurry to cloak the valley in darkness. Without forgetting myself, examining the already darkened faces to see if I could spot Roberto, I followed what people were saying and doing. Three men went forward, one of

them being Canuto. They returned, some minutes later. And Canuto said:

"We battered the door down. It wasn't easy. I swear, as soon as we came away, they went in. A black flock, famished. We pulled the door shut and fastened it from the outside. Not a one will escape, I swear." Extending his arms, he exclaimed:

"Listen!"

Everyone held back, as night's shadows deepened, but the wind's blasts were strong. It whistled among the dry branches, whipping our faces. There came with it, perfectly distinct, the sound of wings. Without seeing, we could visualize. The space scant, the ceiling low, they were still not aware of their prison. But—and by then in the dense shadows—we understood that, having devoured the body, they were trying to escape. We could hear their wings beating in their short limited flights, some colliding with others, blind in the darkness, the skeleton the only white spot. They met the walls, the floor, the ceiling. They would fall back, dazed, and start over. The floor, the ceiling, the walls. And the sound that the wind brought us conveyed the certainty that Gemar Quinto no longer existed, nor his disease.

Slowly, without haste, the men went away, indifferent once more, like strangers. With the road now deserted and the trees bent by the wind, my thoughts were always of Jeronimo and I did not feel the loneliness. The sound of wings attracted me, the mantle of night tranquilized me. I approached the leper's cabin, oblivious of the wind, and, for the first time, my hands were groping for his door. Had it not been for the road, so much with me at that moment, I would have stayed there, innocent of everything, listening to the agony of those wings. I withdrew, however, walking the road once more—but Rosalia's image had already taken Jeronimo's place in my thoughts.

The door yielded, when I pushed it. In my ears, despite the wind, still the sound of wings. On my lips, as if Jeronimo were present, my reply: "It's not necessary." I closed the door, orienting myself in the dark, in search of the lantern. As I made my way, groping along the walls, Rosalia's image was not displaced but remained like a direct vision. It went out when I lit the wick. The light, striking me in the eyes, awoke my senses. I inhaled the air heavy with the smell of oil. Stronger still, deep in the night, the sound of the wings. "Gemar Quinto, a skeleton," I thought. "Bones?" I asked myself, my sense of touch alive to the bail of the lantern. And my voice exploded, aloud, like someone else's, without startling me: "Rosalia's bones." I held up the lantern and went into the sitting room.

Strange indeed, these eyes of mine. They spied the tip of the halter, still on the rafter. The ladder, on the floor. The splotches of blood, also on the floor. I walked past it all rather in haste, as if someone were calling me from the bedroom and, when I came to a stop, I immediately became aware of the rats in the bed. They scampered, in fright, large and repulsive. I put the lantern in the customary place—the sound of the wings still reaching me—, but my eyes once more betrayed me. They stared, against the will of my entire body, precisely at the piece of floor where the dirt was freshest. Underneath, Rosalia. Her teeth, hair, bones. Upon my face, coming to life again, Jeronimo's cuffs and blows like the kicks of an animal. He was pommeling me, violently, his shouts drowning out the sound of the wings, while my teeth bit down upon my lips. Someone, other than I—perhaps more Jeronimo than myself—got down on his knees, with hands cupped, as if to dig. I resisted, everything around me in a flux, at an absolute end, but I resisted as if by miracle. Involuntarily, however, I went over to Rosalia's suitcase, sat down on it, bent over, hiding my face in my hands. They smelled of sweat, these hands, but I had my eyes closed.

All alone, in the black of night, but Rosalia near me. Also near me Gemar Quinto in his sealed cabin. Not far away, the wind, the trees in the valley, the sound of the wings now getting softer. At the roots of my eyes, however, the perfect place for chaotic impressions, Rosalia's brothers were taking shape, suspended as on scales. Roberto, his wide leather belt. Henrique, his swarthy face. Fernando, who was dragging himself, like the crippled dog. In a gang, they were forcing their sister to a sense of violent revulsion, and her hands were now clenched, disembodied in space, like plants scorched by fire. Still the faint, ever so faint, sound of the wings. The tepid sweat on my brow. I stood up, quickly, almost stumbling. My breathing was steady, however. I listened to it with excitement, almost with pleasure, finding in it something human that in myself no longer existed. I flared my nostrils, like an animal, snorting. But there came from within me a warmth that was like a fever, provoking a monstrous indifference to everything around me. It was then that I sought the knife in my belt. I had forgotten it at Jeronimo's cavern.

Jeronimo would bring it the next day, perhaps. At that moment, my final logical and objective thought. Once in the sitting room, I raised the ladder, took down the tip of the halter, and fastened it at my waist, around my belt. I did everything unconsciously, automatically, my nerve cells almost not reacting. My feeling of emptiness, however, endured.

When I went out, I left the door open. The road, the dry ground, the trees, the sky and the open space, all had been transformed into a kind of cloud that the shadows could not obscure. A smoky haze was rising and, crossing it as though an impenetrable veil, I no doubt looked like a specter in a realm of the dead. I had completely forgotten corporeal forms, the faces of men; and the vast silence that enveloped me lay outside any other human experience. I would not believe in a voice if I heard one. If wounded, I would not feel pain. It was written, however, that the night would not be eternal.

My body heat was gone with the still gray light of morning. My lips were parched, my throat inflamed, my legs exhausted. As soon as my great tranquillity had passed, I was reminded of Gemar Quinto and of his cabin. My memory went about reviving, one after another, the pieces of the world. After Gemar Quinto, my house and Rosalia. Next, Jeronimo. Finally, straight in front of my eyes, the road. And always the sound, the almost imperceptible sound of the wings.

Should I keep going, I would once more come to Jeronimo's cavern. Should I turn back, I would walk through the door I had left open. Then, although I was hungry, I drew near the slough —drew quite close, right up to the bank, and stood looking at the stagnant mud, black and sticky. The flies were buzzing. It was giving off a faint vapor. The smell of the muck made me a bit sick. But I lay down on the bare earth, tremendously tired, and before long was fast asleep.

When I awoke, before I could think of myself, I thought of Roberto. Like me, he was an offspring of the valley. He must have known that I would hunt him till he died, day and night, without letup, implacable and cruel. His face, with its huge perverse mouth, replaced the image of Rosalia. I would see it, in the future, every minute of the day. Made in my likeness, like me a victim of the valley, he was not unaware that he had to kill me to stay alive. Dogs, both of us, urged on by the shade of Rosalia.

He was spying on me, no doubt. He was following me, at a distance. In the valley, oftentimes, one man kills while the other sleeps.

This realization came to me when I found Jeronimo sitting on the bed in my bedroom. He was whittling, with my knife, on a piece of wood. Seeing me enter, he looked straight at me, his gaze hard. His hair was longer, his chest bare. He extended his hand, pointing toward the kitchen.

"I brought some clabber and manioc flour," he said.

Jeronimo, always Jeronimo. More than my shadow, more than I myself; faithful and attentive, never for a moment did he stay away. He got up, and I accompanied him, walking out. In the kitchen, he handed me the clay bowl with the clabber and manioc. I stuck my hand in the bowl, licked my fingers, swallowing. His eyes still upon me, his gaze still hard, he added:

"I too saw the end of Gemar Quinto."

The clabber was bitter in my mouth. The beat of my heart was calmer. I was merely eating and, as I ate, listening. Jeronimo bit down on the tip of his knife—which was a habit of mine—and, without averting his eyes, continued:

"I saw you at the leper's door. I was nearby when you entered and left your house. Outside, I stayed with you till you lay down and went to sleep. Someone came sneaking up, as if materializing out of the ground."

"Who?" I cried, the bowl empty.

"Roberto," he replied without changing his tone of voice.

There was a fatal gap. From Jeronimo to me the distance was minimal. But from me to Jeronimo the distance was already enormous, perhaps greater than the valley itself. He could have done what I alone was duty-bound to do. He might perchance have caught Rosalia's brother, and, remembering Rosalia, might have strangled him, in a fit of indignation at seeing him so cowardly. To kill a man who was asleep would be, for Jeronimo, a more abject crime than overpowering one's own sister in order to violate her. His face, however, showed no sign of torment, the intonation of his voice was unchanged, and the sternness of his glance told me that Roberto was still alive. My lips began to close, and Jeronimo continued:

"Roberto turned around when he heard my footsteps. He did not run, Alexandre. He came to me, in silence, and took hold of my arm. We walked, together, not talking. When we were unable to awaken you, and when the smell of the mud in the slough was no longer with us, he stopped to talk. He made me want to vomit, Roberto did. But I listened to what he said, and said straightforwardly, without seeming to lie. A man who swore no oaths, Alexandre, but was shouting the truth."

"What kind of truth?" I inquired.

Jeronimo came closer, so close I could feel his breath. As he got closer, his face grew and his breath came stronger. He was now transcending himself, superior to all things. It was as if I were hearing Roberto himself. Axe blows, his words. He was seized by the trance that always marks the faces of those who are dying. Reaching me through him, his most faithful messenger, came the other's confession.

"Roberto is innocent," he exclaimed, without hesitation," completely innocent!"

"Innocent, do you mean innocent?"

" 'I had no one I could speak to,' these were Roberto's words" —Jeronimo paused for a second, but did not become impassioned, and he resumed with a more resonant voice: "Listen,

Alexandre, I implore you. Listen, because Rosalia is going to be reborn. You didn't know her, nor did I know her, the Ouro Valley did not know her."

Looking me in the eye, he sternly pronounced the judgment: "Another woman is going to emerge from her death. Another woman, Alexandre. Another woman, I repeat, if indeed she ever reached the state of being human."

Snatching the bowl from my hands, he took me by the arm. Perhaps I was, for him, at that moment, the child of days past. He guided me like a father, and, now in the yard, the warmth of his voice still upon his lips, he slowed me to point out a man who was waiting for me. As if opening my unseeing eyes, abruptly quieting my inner convulsion, Jeronimo said:

"It's Roberto, her brother."

I would have killed Roberto under any other circumstances, if perchance I had met him an hour earlier. Jeronimo, however, had frustrated my wrath. He had put aside, while I ate, the hatred that Rosalia had forced on me like a poison. He had ripped the shadowy veil that still enveloped me and the muffled cry finally made my body shudder: "Had Rosalia lied?" Logic was returning afresh, a closed chain of question marks, while my eyes were probing and my hands would not keep still. "Was it all a lie?" The knife in her hands, her father's death struggle, the dog, Roberto brandishing the strap. Her words took on a physical quality. I could once more see her lacerated thighs. I could once more hear her moans uttered without tears. "If it all had been a lie, who was Rosalia?" One question, however, remained. The big question, I didn't know if anyone could answer: "Her child, who was the father of her child?" Roberto was at hand, I knew well enough. And, in between us, fairer than truth itself, was Jeronimo.

It seemed to me, suddenly, that everything in Roberto's face was striving desperately to maintain composure. Slowly, however, I began to perceive that something, harbored in the flash of his glance, was reaching me. The terror, the human terror in the depths of his eyes. It was not base; in any case it did not emerge as an uncontrollable impulse, it did not occur in the least like something in a nightmare. Monstrous, almost, like the terror of a snake writhing on a bed of coals. It irritated me. It made me gnash my teeth precisely because it transformed him from a cruel animal into a man who, because of his sister, was suffering the profound consciousness of his guilt. I lowered my gaze, seeking his fingers. They were not stained with the blood of the birds. Impossible for me to believe now—looking into the face that I finally discovered to be so similar to Rosalia's—that he could have hurt anything at all. The certainty, which before had come to me through Jeronimo, grew stronger. He would rather permit his own death, offering himself as a sacrifice, than have to strike or harm someone. The foremost of his enemies would be spared, he would bless me myself if I killed him, but his arm would be incapable of self-defense—much less of attack! And the entire reaction that his presence provoked in me brought to my lips the unuttered exclamation: "This man is innocent." I had never been drunk, to be sure, but my head swam as if I were drunk.

He would soon be speaking, as he had spoken to Jeronimo. Brief pauses would ensue while, in the floor of the bedroom, Rosalia's bones would crackle under the force of his final confession. Had she been alive, perhaps she would have run at that instant, with her child in her arms, to hurl herself into the muddy slough. Now that she was dead, her brother's voice would snap like a whip. But the animosity that separated me from him having been dispelled, Jeronimo bringing us together with his heavy hands, things were still unclear to me because the terror in his eyes was insufficient to explain his sister's fate.

I looked, in anticipation, for his first word. Awaiting it, I pondered what might have happened to me had not Jeronimo watched over my sleep and had not Roberto come. He would be speaking, without delay, in a moment. I shrank back, nearly losing my footing, until I felt the wall of the house behind me. My hands were trembling against the harshness of the brick.

PART THREE

MY HANDS TREMBLE EVEN NOW, but the bricks have turned black with the smoke from the fire. Their roughness is different. As brutal as in the old days, as useless now as my own past, my hands grope over them. If it were possible, at this moment, I would return without them. I would let them remain, nailed to the wall, like pieces of still living flesh. Nevertheless, the wind has not subsided, the black sky seems to have lowered, and I am the only creature who, midst the dew, breathes the air that should belong only to the trees and shrubs. Except for my eyes, shining like those of an animal, there is only the lantern light. Seen from above, it will appear to be a star on the ground.

And from the light that floats out, faint and shimmering, I seem to see tongues of fire springing up. The flames, transparent, emerge simultaneously from all sides, so that I may see it all turned to ashes, the wood crackling, Jeronimo from the mouth of his cavern sensing in the rising smoke how men never forgive the innocent. Invincible fire that feeds and spreads, ever devouring, and goes out when there is nothing left to burn. A hellish firebrand, with towering flames, that saves the walls and especially spares the dirt floor.

The earth is virgin once more. Gone are footprints, every human vestige is expunged, and what reappears is the primitive crust of the valley. Rosalia, however, is still asleep in its pit. If the heat of the flames are reaching her, I do not know. But I do know that, awakening and awake, I have a presentiment that Jeronimo will not be long in coming. I bend over, take hold of the lantern, close my eyes. The resounding of the wings, now. Only for a moment, a brief moment, because immediately there arises, in the little circle of light, the desolation that surrounds me.

Do not go away yet, I beg you. Observe that, in the layers of charred rubble, I am attempting to locate the bedroom. The walls keep disorienting me. I go back and forth, walking slowly, over earth unvaryingly even. Slowly I reconstruct the architecture. With my feet, I try to measure the distances. Finally I locate where the bed was and, pausing, make my calculations painstakingly. I draw near, retracing my steps of times past, and I cannot prevent my lips from saying: "Here is where it was." On the dirt surface there is not the least scar. The earth is compact and hard. The air cannot penetrate it, the wind's echo cannot sink in, it does not in the least perceive the weight of my body. Between it and me, at this moment, rather than an absurd conflict, the struggle being waged is that of insensibility against the willpower of a madman. I hold my breath, prick up my ears—

but I cannot hear it as nothing comes from inside, no worm is crawling, no vapor is being given off, its rigidity monstrously inscrutable. If it could speak, I would ask it questions. I would require a complete confession, how it absorbed the blood and stripped the breast of flesh, and spared the bones, in the slow ritual of extermination. Whether there was pain, whether her arms did not twist around her trunk, grotesquely, trying to protect her remains from inexorable corruption. It was not, however, endowed with voice.

I draw away, fearing that time will rout the night, already afraid lest I be seen, I who should have been burned with my house, my pigs, my land. But the shadows are dense. Morning, far away. Alone in this remoteness, it is still possible for me to contemplate the valley now devoid of magnitude, its boundaries restricted, its entire presence concentrated between the blackened walls. I am aware that the wind blasts are strong. What comes hurtling, parting the shadows to find me, is the anguished shout of a man.

I lean back against the wall, in order not to fall. I close my eyes in order not to see. I am betrayed by my poor hands, trembling and ill-fated. And the shout comes alive, as physical as Jeronimo's blows on my face.

"No one knows why she was that way," said Roberto, as if he were not beginning but rather continuing his confession, "and no one will ever know how she came by her perverse heart. A perverse heart, it was. You can talk to my brothers, you can go back to our house and I'll show you all the things she did. My mother never knew her. She was raised, you might say, by my father and, being quite a bit younger than we, she would kick and cry when we tried to take her up in our arms. Her main diversion, until she got older, had always been her own hair. She would pull out hairs and burn them in the fire. She spoke only rarely. She would become absolutely quiet when Father came home. She kept away from him as if he were a monster.

"When Rosalia got older, and had a bed of her own, we lost our last remnant of tranquillity. She seemed to care nothing for sleep, this girl. She would light the hearth fire, constantly feeding it wood, and many were the nights we found her thus: sitting in front of the flames, her gaze vacant, as if oblivious of herself. When she caught sight of us, she would run. Before Father decided to take her with us to our work, her chief distraction during the day took place not in the house but rather on the bank of the slough.

"The slough is not far from the house, it is true. It is also true that no one ever comes by there. Except for cactus, nothing but rocks and hard ground. But there are rats, I can tell you. Rosalia would catch them in the traps she brought from home and, when she did not kill them with her bare hands, she threw them into the muck. She took pleasure in seeing the rats die slowly, struggling in the sticky stuff, swallowed by the black mud. Had she a child, I swear, she would have been capable of hurling it into that muck.

"It was later, however, that she began to think about the birds. Father had some cages there at home. She took the birds out, one by one, and, with her knife, cut off their legs. With the point, she put out the eyes of two or three, I don't quite recall. Father got angry, of course. He even beat her, Father did, so hard that

Rosalia vomited blood. I came to her aid and never shall forget what she did then. She put her hand in the blood and sniffed it. She wouldn't let me wash it off, and the blood dried on her fingers, I swear. The following night, I was asleep and woke up to hear Father screaming. When I came running, she passed by me with a piece of burning wood in her hands. Father's face was burned raw. And he was moaning. She had entered his room, with the brand afire, and had slammed it full force into Father's face. If she wanted to kill him, I don't know. But I swear that, though he did not lose his sight, Father was transformed into something horrendous. You have seen his face, Father's face, and will remember.

"She lost her speech, then. If we spoke, she didn't answer. She would lock herself in her room, at first all alone and later with the dog. She started by cutting off its tail. Later, she cut off its ears. And Father whipped her again with the belt, nearly out of his mind. Did she cry? Not at all. Nor did she faint, I swear it. But she began to fix herself up. Now she would clean her nails, wash her clothes, comb her hair. She insisted on going with us to the harvests. And that's how she met Chico Viegas, the potter's son. Chico Viegas, that is, Canuto's son. A strange fellow, that one. Once he came by the house, with old Canuto. Clearly he had not come by choice but rather had been dragged by the old man, who seemed to be interested in seeing his son take a wife. A bit daft is what he was, this Chico Viegas. He preferred to spend his time working in the clay, silent and suspicious. Possibly Canuto saw in Rosalia a kind of salvation for his son. Possibly, that is. The girl could bring the boy to life, help end his simple-mindedness. Possibly. But, when the matter came up, Father could not hide the panic he felt.

"I can see him now, talking. Burned and shriveled, his skin

makes one think of a toad's. His lips, which have shrunk, no longer cover up his teeth. What he is saying, however, is very precise and weighs heavily upon the room: 'Boys, Rosalia hates everything that lives.' He lowers his arms, not blinking an eye, and adds: 'She will do to men what she did to birds, to rats, to the dog.' And he concludes, firmly: 'She should have been dropped in the forest, like the young of animals.' A perverse heart, I swear. That is why he holds Chico Viegas off. But he will use Chico Viegas to keep away the others who may appear. He becomes the suitor on whose account his daughter stays at home, watched, followed, at bay. His daughter should not come in contact with anyone with her evil nature, her cobra instincts. He feared she might do to a stranger what she did to him, her father.

"We, Fernando, Henrique, and I, thought like Father. Rosalia was capable of the worst. But she had one quality, let me say. She loved horses. She would let them eat corn out of her hands. She washed them almost every day, wasting the water. For a horse, let me tell you, she would be willing to suffer. And willing to suffer only for a horse, you can bet. Much of her time was spent there, among them. She didn't ride them, however. Why she preferred them, I don't know. Nor did Father know, nor Fernando, nor Henrique. Perhaps she envied their strength, their muscles. But she never missed the harvests; as we could not leave her to herself, Father permitted her to accompany us.

"You appeared, at that moment. She of course told us many things. Rosalia, bear in mind, invented a great deal. She lied just for the pleasure of lying. What she told you, I can imagine. But the truth is that, to Rosalia, you meant no more than Chico Viegas. Rosalia just wanted a man. Someone to take her away from her father, perhaps. In my opinion, however, she wanted someone to help her get revenge. Father would not escape alive, she had sworn to herself. Chico Viegas would not do. You, on the other hand, appeared at the right moment.

"The blame, let me say, was not yours. Father was to blame. He had always hoped to avoid the worst, that Rosalia might, while out of his sight, terrorize the valley. Rosalia hated everything. Except for the horses, as I said. And that is why Father did not want her to be away. But he could not explain it to a stranger and, furthermore, Chico Viegas was his argument. He used this argument on you, I know. You resisted, I also know. And that night, when you challenged him, when he jumped on you, Rosalia was spying. I did not see it, but I swear she was spying. She was always spying, she spied on everything, Rosalia did. A snake under your heel would not have had its eyes more wide open.

"Our father was a strong man. A man who could lift a tree with his arms. If angered, he could throw a bull by the horns. Even armed as you were, even if there were ten of you, he would win easily. From the front, I give you my word, no knife on earth could touch him. He was always getting in fights. When I saw him dead, the dog licking his blood, my first act was to locate the wound. Delivered by treachery, the stab was in the back of course. You, whom he could see, could not have done it—who could have done it? In the kitchen, Rosalia was washing her hands. I didn't threaten her. Nor did Enrique or Fernando. But Father's body was to her a matter of as much indifference as the slop.

"A dead man, even if he is your father, is not worth much. Carrion, that's all. He can't walk, can't talk, can't suffer. But the following day Rosalia had no more feeling for him than she had for the body of the dog. She killed the dog, herself, the same night. How she killed it, I don't know. You had been at the house, a few minutes before, and we made it clear she had to stay. Above all she had to attend the burial. Fernando picked up the bloody animal and left in a big hurry. He went to the slough and dropped the dog into the ooze. When he returned, in silence as always, for Fernando doesn't talk, he found us in the living room; Henrique was cutting tobacco, and I was waiting for you and Jeronimo. Getting her things together, Rosalia acted as if nothing had happened. Had you arrived at that moment, I should have explained everything. Jeronimo of course came much later, and when he came, my attitude was as you observed.

"There was nothing more to do, I believe. One thing, however, perhaps the remembrance of Father, led me to find out what was happening between Rosalia and you. I began to hang around the house and was not long in discovering that Rosalia was ill. How she had gotten ill, I don't know. But I made a new discovery, too. Gemar Quinto, the leper, was also hanging around the house. Once, in Jeronimo's absence, the leper got in. I dashed for the kitchen, reached the sitting room, pressed my ear to the wall. She was calling to the leper with open arms. Unable to contain myself, I entered the bedroom, with a shout.

"The earth, which swallowed up her perverse heart, have pity on her flesh. Her eyes were blazing like the valley sun. Her bare breasts danced. A rabid dog, I assure you, would have been more human. I cried out again, like a madman. The leper recoiled, and dragging himself, left the house. We were alone, Rosalia and I. She wasn't expecting me, certainly, but she showed no surprise. Her lips twisted, and I could tell that her rage was intense. She leaned against the wall as she sat down on the bed. 'He will bleed you like a stuck pig,' she said, her excitement rising. I approached her, I, her brother, and inquired: 'But why did you tempt Gemar Quinto?' She pulled up her skirt, exposing her thighs, before reply. At that moment, despite the certainty that she was my sister, I knew that Rosalia was not a woman. If she could bite, she would have. Her words came, decisively. An explosion, that is. I can still hear her and I shall never forget what she said, what she revealed as if she were vomiting blood: 'He thinks I am pregnant, he, Alexandre. He thinks the child is yours, Roberto. I violated myself, tore my own flesh with my nails. They hurt, they burn, these stinking sores! But he, Alexandre, will bleed all of you dry. You will all end up like Father.' The urge that beset me was to close her mouth with my fist. Had Father been there, in my place, he would have torn out her tongue. But Rosalia exclaimed: 'Do you want to know then why I called to Gemar Quinto! Do you want to know? Very well! I wanted his disease, I wanted his leprosy to transmit to Alexandre, to Jeronimo, I wanted to see the valley come to the same end, swollen, rotten, disintegrating. I did, Roberto, I still do!' She tried to get up, to get out of bed, but before she could do so, I left the room. I abandoned your house, I give you my word.

"With Rosalia alive, I knew you would not listen to me. But she, for her part, would not kill herself. She would sacrifice you, me, Fernando, and Henrique. The person who should have killed her, and strangled her like something unworthy of living, was her own father, my father. He did not. It fell to me, her oldest brother, to put an end to her wicked heart. Mine the obligation to be the killer of my sister. Not out of pity, I assure you. To kill my sister out of duty, to remove a threat to our very lives. Henrique would perhaps be opposed. Perhaps Fernando would be opposed. I made my preparations, then, in silence.

"I acquainted myself intimately with your habits, Alexandre. I followed Jeronimo's footsteps like a shadow. And I caught Rosalia, finally, that afternoon. There was no time to speak. There was no time for our eyes to meet. She was standing, at the stove, with her back to me. Hearing the sound of my feet, close behind her, she tried to turn around. I struck her on the head with a piece of firewood. A stout blow it was. My sister tottered, trying to maintain her balance. I struck her again, still harder. And Rosalia, my sister, fell. The flames in the fireplace made my face flush and my blood boil. I, however, was busy thinking. I had already thought of throwing the body in the muddy slough. That's what she used to do with the rats. But I saw the halter, I tell you. Up in the ceiling, I saw the rafter and I thought of the gallows. It was a matter of but a moment to turn thought to action. I steadied the ladder, tied the halter around the rafter, fashioned the noose. It was not easy to carry the body up the ladder; she was very heavy, my sister was. Resting her body on the ladder itself, I finally managed to put her neck through the noose. I gave my sister's body a push, after that. And the leather held, fortunately. I got down, put the ladder back where I had found it, and, keeping behind those rocks, waited for you to come back. You, however, were delayed.

"The next day, I was very busy. I went to the foot of the mountain, with Henrique, to see if we could catch some goats. On the way back, Henrique asked about his sister. I said merely that she had died. I also told Fernando, back home, that his sister was dead. Neither one nor the other gave it much importance, as if it were something quite natural. I had done, after all, what Father would have done. Only two days afterward, however, I remembered my sister's confession. You, Alexandre, might have thought that she killed herself on account of the child. You of course had believed Rosalia, my sister. She was pure wickedness.

"With my sister dead, you would blame me. My sister managed you, Alexandre. She had said that I violated her. She had maintained that I was the father of her child. With my sister dead, you would try to kill me, I knew. It was my duty to kill my sister, the soul of wickedness, but not to kill you, Alexandre. If I killed you, Alexandre, I would be despicable. But not my sister—she deserved to die. I killed her, and that's why. I did my duty. I would kill my sister again, I give you my word.

"I saw you sleeping, Alexandre. You were tired, I could easily see. But what I wanted was to tell you all this, tell the truth, blow by blow as one fells a tree. Jeronimo, however, came along. Jeronimo did not want me to awaken you. He took me some distance from here, Jeronimo did. And, while you slept, I told Jeronimo what I have now told you. Think what you will, you can be certain of one thing—Rosalia, my sister, hated you, me, Jeronimo, the whole valley. The only things our sister did not hate were the horses. She hated men, she hated life, even. Wherever it may be, Rosalia's blood will nourish, deep among the rocks and roots, her eternal hatred of men and of life. The best thing is to forget, Alexandre, as Henrique and Fernando have done.

"My sister's wicked heart, Alexandre, is in need of silence."

Only my ears were aware—far away the valley wind, closer the barking of dogs, closer still my own breathing. Then, Roberto's face. I felt the challenge of his eyes, his teeth, his nostrils, his sweaty brow, and his mouth wet with saliva. At my side, Jeronimo, constant and changeless shadow, as if he were the house's most unyielding wall. In the yard, steady on the dry ground, our bare feet were moving. I sought to raise my eyes, to look straight at the man who had just spoken, but when I did, I encountered two calloused hands that were guarding his face against my astonishment.

He put his hands down, now silent. No longer could I learn what lay behind his mask. Impassive, he was waiting for me. But I, who for my part should either have attacked or blessed him, once again waited for Jeronimo. My father's friend, however, did not speak. Chewing his tobacco, his bull neck unmoving, Jeronimo gave Roberto a chance to say:

"The valley knows nothing."

"Nothing?" Jeronimo repeated, inquiringly.

"Nothing—no," he replied, "the valley knows that my sister died from hanging."

"Who said so?" asked Jeronimo.

Roberto raised his hand, pointed in the direction of Gemar Quinto's house, and replied:

"We were questioned."

As I heard the dialogue, I was vaguely taking part in it. "A man can lie," I managed to think, with great effort. "He can lie especially when a dead woman is the accuser"—boldly, ideas and images were battling within me. Back and forth, on the end of the rope, Rosalia's body swinging. Then, laid out, in the floor. The recollection that came next was that of the mare that Jeronimo slaughtered for jerked meat, a long time ago, when I was still at his cavern. Blood was smeared on his hands, arms, chest. And in those hands, which were ripping out intestines and cleaning out the belly, a repugnant mass, still without shape, caught my eye. Jeronimo exclaimed: "Pregnant, the mare was!" He added, looking at me: "This would have been a foal!" I kept going over it in my mind, as the remembrance was fading, and I was once more seeing Roberto, and I began to feel it would be unworthy of me not to verify the truth. I looked straight at Jeronimo, seeking his support, and begged:

"Come with me, Jeronimo," and louder, "let him come with us."

As if understanding my hallucination—which at that instant was like the delirium of one who seeks to know the truth—Roberto recoiled, trying to run, attempting perhaps to get away. He was impelled less by his own instincts than by the determination that could be read on my face. I must have been, at that moment, like the Luna brothers. Brutalized, like the lowliest creature in the valley. My bare chest covered with dirt, my heavy hands filthy, my clothes smelling of sweat. But Roberto restrained himself, as strong as his own father.

"Let's go," he said.

We entered the house slowly, in no hurry, as if directed by some superior force. Jeronimo continued to chew tobacco. Roberto did not hesitate. And when I strode into the bedroom, with its closed window, I was not surprised by the wooden bed. If she had been in it, Rosalia herself would not have surprised me. What did surprise me was to feel myself on the verge of violating the dead—of seeking the truth in its physical testimony, of going after it in the pit of a womb that perhaps no longer existed. I would have recoiled, inevitably recoiled, had Roberto not been at my side and had Jeronimo not reflected, in his voice, that firmness that was always a command.

"Bring me the hoe, the hoe and the shovel," I heard—it was Jeronimo's voice.

I had left them, in the bedroom, on my way to the sitting room. Gripping my stomach anew, hunger joined in increasing my agitation. It was hard for me to breathe, my fatigue grew, and the daylight itself turned redder than the clay of the valley. I returned, however, with the hoe and the shovel. And without

Roberto's making the least move, Jeronimo once again took my place. He had surmised all I had thought. He did what it was mine to do.

The chop of the hoe into the ground—the first, second, third —the valley again turning into a furnace. Sweat poured off us, as the hoe rose and fell, all thought having vanished. Our arms, Roberto's and mine, hung limp, but I felt as if my hands were supported by solid rock. We stood there, our blood circulating feverishly, waiting for Jeronimo to stop. And we waited, the valley boiling, hotter than our sweat, Jeronimo now stripped of his shirt, his muscular chest like the thorax of a horse.

"The shovel, now!" shouted Jeronimo.

Roberto stepped close, the dirt Jeronimo was removing falling at our feet. I was beginning to see, to glimpse in the moister earth the testimony we were looking for—and it was when Roberto bent down, the smell of corruption having mingled with the valley heat, that Jeronimo began to be afraid his shovel might cut into the flesh rooted in the earth. Enormous, with his legs hidden in the grave, his chest naked, the shovel upraised, Jeronimo searched in my eyes for my steadfast collaboration. He was not a man asking, but the accomplice who had guessed all. He inquired, however, coldly:

"Is it still worth while?"

He cleaned his mouth with his dirt encrusted hand, the muscles tight in his huge arms. Upon me, as always, his staring eyes. He shook his head, his hair dancing upon his shoulders, and then said:

"We will have to take it out in pieces."

It was then that I understood—and only then that I understood that it was all in vain. Too late, in fact. The corpse seemed to have exploded when the weight of the earth was removed, organs and clay intermingling, only the heat and the putridness revealing the flesh already without blood or shape. Had Jeronimo gotten down and tried to remove the veil of earth from her face, her features would surely have burst out of the shape that immobility itself maintained. Down there it was impossible to establish the absolute truth. Death was in league with the earth to strengthen one man's deposition. But something was pushing me to my limit.

Without my calling him, Jeronimo jumped up out of the grave. Irrespirable, the air. The sweat was running in the hair of our chests. In my memory, the valley having faded, arose the image of the hand I had seen when the body had toppled down from the rafter. I sought it, in the bottom, beneath a thin layer of earth. And I found it, almost unrecognizable, a few fingers with no flesh, but still curving, as alive as my own hand. I felt, upon my lips, the grimace of rage. And, before Jeronimo could pick up the shovel, I had the sudden urge to force her brother's definitive confession in the presence of Rosalia's rotting corpse. Jeronimo, as always, was foresighted. It was he who pointed the way and who for my sake provoked in Roberto the suspicion that we now, and as always, believed the dead woman. I had heard his confession, but Rosalia had also made hers. Unable to see beyond the words, unable to know who was lying, I was led to Roberto by something in my nature that was destroying my entire inner being. A rabbit, still alive in a dog's mouth, could not have been more frightened. The blood reddened his face, already dripping with sweat, his eyes were ablaze—but the stench of carrion was impelling me beyond my ability to restrain my feet. Impassive spectator, Jeronimo folded his arms.

Approaching Roberto, who was waiting with his back to the wall, I could hear the excruciating voice of Rosalia. I kept hearing it, my memory stronger than her body, and I could see her brother prone over her. I held myself back, knowing that the open grave was beside me, and I cannot even say, rationally, if mine was the voice that exclaimed:

"She was carrying a child!"

And I screamed, sweaty, hungry, innocent, and unaccountable for all my acts:

"Your child!"

Roberto's mind was gone, I could tell. His eye saw, his ear heard, his touch sensed—but, accused by me, and I already a phantom, beneath the ground the rotting foetus of his own child, he was losing his mind because only a mindless man would be capable of doing what he did. He pointed his hand at the grave and said:

"Some day, attracted by this woman, the mountains will walk. They will walk, like giants, and they will bury the valley."

But I stifled this threat, not with a blow to his mouth, but by choking his windpipe with hands that, no longer mine, belonged to the memory of Rosalia that guided me. I was sickened by the foul air. Even more, I was intoxicated by the asphyxiation of the open mouth, the vile teeth, the filthy tongue. I should have used torture and forced a path for truth through physical pain, and, if he said nothing, I should have torn out his tongue and thrown it in the open grave so that Rosalia might feel it palpitating in the warmth of her putrefaction. I struck him in the stomach with my knee, a hard blow. When he fell, at the edge of the grave, what bothered me most was the remains of my wife's body, almost hidden in the earth. Struck dumb, although Jeronimo encouraged me with his unforgiving gaze, I would have let myself be overcome by Roberto, in his rage, had not my father's friend kicked him in the face. Bending down, Jeronimo placed in my hand my own knife. A creature cut loose from everything at that instant, without a single repressed instinct, absolutely free. Spontaneously came the impulse that, steadying my hand, brought down the knife. I had aimed for his eyes, and I hit them in two quick gouges with the sharp point. He shuddered, screaming, possessed at that moment of inhuman strength. A shove against my chest made me waver. And, when I looked up, the air utterly foul and hot, the man leaping before me had now become the raving specter of grief and damnation.

My victim had no name. Pressing against his eye sockets, now two holes from which blood was running and deforming his face, his fists sought in vain to stanch the shooting pain in his eyes that had made him jump. Blinded, still on his feet because the pain was holding him up, he terrified me as if Rosalia's own body, rising out of the earth, had come alive and spoken. This tremendous apparition was, however, short-lived. Moved perhaps less by mercy than by the animal instinct of fear of death, Jeronimo went to him, impassive as ever, and tightened his hands around his neck. In the silence that had fallen, the faint breath on his lips sounded as loud as a shot:

"I told the truth," he whispered.

But, as I looked on, the muscles of Jeronimo's arms grew rigid. Then, I saw his fall. And I heard the voice:

"The man is dead."

The first moments were not difficult. Jeronimo, his hands bloody, was breathing and reacting as if nothing had happened. He wiped his hands on the hair of his chest and, seeing me cowering, almost overcome by the foul air, with my clouded gaze barely noticing the open grave, Roberto's still warm body, he slowly came over to me. He seized me by the hair and dragged me away to the sitting room, then to the kitchen. He went out, returning immediately. He raised the wooden bowl he had brought and dashed the cold water over me. Next he lit a fire and, in an earthen pot, put water on to boil. He then told me, handing me a piece of lemon he had already sliced:

"Suck it, the sourness will do you good."

I took the lemon in my mouth, totally exhausted, my stomach racked with hunger. Reclining I remained, my eyes closed, sucking the lemon as if I were a baby sucking its mother's breast. But, though only my hearing was functioning, I was aware of reality around me—I heard Jeronimo's steps going away, and I was not long in verifying that, in the bedroom, he was back at work with the shovel. I put my ear to the ground. One by one, for a long time, I followed the movements of the shovel. At last, coinciding with the final stroke of the shovel, Jeronimo's footsteps. And his question, which was unexpected, made me open my eyes:

"Do you feel better?"

"And Roberto," I asked, "what was done with Roberto?"

Jeronimo pointed to the bedroom with his hand and replied: "I'll tell his brothers. They will come and get him."

He picked me up and, when I was on my feet, gave me the pants and shirt that he had brought from the bedroom. Led by him, I went to the kitchen area in the back. I washed and put on the pants and shirt, but Jeronimo, for all his searching, could find nothing for us to eat. There was still time for us to return to the cavern and, before afternoon, Jeronimo would inform Roberto's brothers. We withdrew from the house, leaving the door open. As we walked along the road, our bodies overheated, heads aching, tasting the bitter saliva, our empty stomachs were a sufficient goad. Hunger hindered any recollections but exaggerated the perfume of earth and leaves.

The fire, however, was alight inside the cavern. I had devoured almost my entire portion of the meat spitted, then roasted over the coals, when Jeronimo gave me the manioc flour. Squatting near the fire, blowing on the embers to encourage the flames, Jeronimo seemed more powerful and less savage. Surrounded by rock walls, under a ceiling likewise of rock, the fire blazing on the floor, I looked straight at Jeronimo—this time controlling myself and certain that he would soon be departing. He turned to me and announced:

"I will go to Roberto's brothers' place. Wait for me. I won't be long."

I lay down on the oxhide, which was his bed, when he left. Overcome by fatigue, my muscles relaxing, I immediately fell asleep. How long I slept I don't recall. I know that my heavy sleep was shattered when Jeronimo pushed open the door violently, the wood slamming against the stone. He had come in haste, it was clear. On his face, stuck to the sweat, the dust of the road. His huge hands, widespread, moved with his words.

"The men of the valley are gathering," he said.

"Why, Jeronimo?" I asked.

"They found Roberto's body, with his eyes gouged out, at your house."

And he exclaimed:

"They're full of hatred, now, these men!"

"Hatred, these men?" I repeated.

Jeronimo's hands shut tight, his feet steadied as if they were roots. His immobile face, however, was as hard as the very rocks that surrounded us. Hoarsely, his voice:

114

"Roberto's brothers took the body from door to door. You had killed the father, you had killed the daughter, you had killed the brother. You, Alexandre, are a condemned man!"

He concluded, observing me:

"They are already cutting the trees for the gallows."

But, before I could reason for myself, Jeronimo came closer. I could see the distended muscles in his bull neck. Fearful lest he lose his voice, for Jeronimo would become mute when the blood rushed to his head, I inquired precipitously:

"And what shall we do?"

The giant, who in his rage appeared neither to see nor to feel, able to hold off the valley with one hand and pull the gallows down with the other, did not hear me. Perhaps he could no longer think. A crazed bitch, hurling herself against the blade of a scythe in defense of her threatened pup, would have more of the human than he. Had he fought, at that moment, and struck someone in the face, he would have disfigured him. With the slightest move, he would have dislocated an arm or a leg from a human body. Stones would have been more feeling, wild beasts less unpitying. Facing him, the valley would have fallen back, would not have dared come near. And whoever might venture, might dare to go in my direction, would not come back on his feet. He was the more human, this Jeronimo, because he was stronger than any animal.

His shirt open, baring his herculean chest, he put his knife in his belt. He picked up a knapsack, in which he put the roast meat and manioc flour, and, handing it to me, he dragged me out of the cavern. I also had my knife in my belt. We then began to walk. Empty and cloudless was the sky, when I gazed at it, my feet on the road. I was not fleeing but leaving the valley, without fear, guided by Jeronimo. At the second curve, on the flat plain where the cactus had become tangled in a knot of spines, we could hear the still faint outcry, which kept growing in volume and in no time became quite loud. They, the inhabitants of the Ouro Valley, were waiting for us.

When we got around the cactus, the earth now giving back to the air the heat received from the sun, we saw close by the very same people who had gathered in front of Gemar Quinto's cabin. They were the same men, the same women. Their dogs snarled. Bursting in our ears, the excited cries. Scythes held in calloused hands, blades flashing in the light, knives being brandished. But, always at my side like a spectral, inhuman father, his hair down over his shoulders, his hands open like iron buckets, Jeronimo kept advancing, deaf and unwavering, oblivious to dangers and insults. At close range, perhaps because they began to see in Jeronimo the challenge of an indomitable animal, everyone grew silent. A few dogs alone kept up their barking.

Roberto's body, however, was there. Like a frontier, sprawled on the road, nearly naked and still bloody, he separated us, Jeronimo and me, from the rest of the valley. One more step and my feet reached his face. Someone, a dark skinned, still youngish man, ran at me, brandishing a long knife. I had plenty of time to clear the inert body because, no sooner had his feet hit the ground than Jeronimo's arms were hauling him up violently, the speed of the attack making the long knife fall to the road. Less than a second, perhaps. The valley men gave way slightly, and suddenly Jeronimo, with a face that anger was turning into a frightening physical mask, was twirling him in the air as if he were a bundle. Bearing him thus, and shouting, he managed to force a crack in the human wall. Knife in hand, I advanced backward, so they would not overtake Jeronimo from the rear. When at last he turned around, the open road now beckoning, everyone saw the thrust of his tremendous arms, the thick muscles tensed, and the man being hurled down to smash against the ground, moaning. Jeronimo then drew his knife and, tossing his hair on his shoulders, turned his huge bull neck.

No one else came close, human mouths were stilled, and there were only the barking dogs. A little more and night would fall, with its dark clouds, the valley retreating, the road guiding us like something alive. We slowly drew away, Jeronimo's eyes probing, alert. We spoke no words, one alongside the other, our feet on the rough ground. Finally, when the nocturnal shadows descended, the bats now taking wing, we gained the valley's desert zone. The naked plain, devoid of houses, of men, of trees. The mountains, however, were far off.

In this stretch, between the desert and the mountains, Jeronimo recalled to me fragments of my past. "A man dies while still alive, Alexandre," he said. He talked, as we walked, for a long time. And when he finished and came to a halt, I understood that the moment had come for him to return, leaving me all alone. Ahead of me, like an invincible obstacle, the mountain. He raised his hand, pointing:

"On the other side is Abilio's world," he said.

He did not shake my hand, nor could I make out even his face in the darkness. Moving away, returning to the valley as if he could not escape his prison, he exclaimed in a voice so strong that it was able to overcome the wind's pounding:

"The powers of fortune go with you!"

A dead man, in his tomb, could not have been more lonely. Above me, the black sky. Down below, the empty plain. Ahead, the mountain. At my back, the road. And for light, only what came from my eyes. Thus submerged, without Jeronimo and the

Ouro Valley, surrounded by cactus and thorns, I began to climb, already tired, in hopes of finding Gemar Quinto's wild goats. I walked and walked, but there was no one around but myself and my fate. As I climbed, I thought the night would never end.

Still without having gained the summit, I lay down to get some sleep. I made a fire by striking two rocks together, the spark falling on tinder. Alongside my little campfire, I rested. My delirium was still far away and my irrepressible memory lay buried deep within me. Thanks to the protection of my cauterized consciousness, I went to sleep. When I awoke, at dawn, I was hungry. I took out the meat Jeronimo had put in the knapsack and ate it. I started walking again, always climbing.

Looking back, hours later, I could not see the valley. There was nothing behind me but the naked rock, barren of vegetation, of animals, of life. If I shouted, my own echo would strangle in the deep silence. Even the wind no longer existed and, overmastered by the rocks, had had to remain down below, at the level of the valley. Slick metallic surface, montage of hot glass, this was a different sky. Nature here was devastating. My feet, however, did not hold back. And I kept up what was not really an advance.

Functioning like a machine out of control, annihilating an almost complete solitude, my memory gave back everything it had just experienced. Bodies got to their feet in the circle of my images. Voices were reborn. Faces could be seen. The valley landscape, however, which my memory revived, finally was destroyed in the face of the new panorama I was beholding. I no longer had to climb—but what I saw was in truth a region petrified. Wild goats could surely not graze there. Nor could men live there.

The rocks, covering the plain, tearing open the earth, were

like sharp teeth filed for cutting. Joined one to the other, as if the earth were a jawbone, they barred the way, rather like a frontier with another universe. Their sparkling points were returning light to the sun. I stopped. And from that moment to this, I have kept alive because I felt the blood in me; the conflict between a destructible body and an ungovernable soul gained momentum. I learned, at that moment, that I could humble the world—simply by going mad and killing reality. First, however, I would have to agonize. And that agony truly began when, barefooted, I set out to make the long, painful crossing. The heat was suffocating, and I could not tell if it came from the sun or from the rocks. My body afire, now without food and racked by thirst, I could feel my lacerated feet, and a trail of blood bespoke the sacrifice of my slow advance. My hands came to my aid but they soon were torn. It would have been useless to cry out and it would have been useless to ask help. But, when the first night fell, the stars ever clearer and my pain more acute, I was sorry I had not let myself be killed in the valley. Dragging myself, hurting, hungry, thirsty, I crawled along—without the least notion whether the rocky plain ever ended or not. Perhaps I was coming up to the doorway of hell.

I did enter hell, no doubt about it. Castigated by the light of day, set upon by the shadows of night, my eyes could no longer distinguish between day and night, light and shadow. I am not sure, therefore, whether it was the third day or the fourth night —I a worm, my beard enormous, my tongue chewed by my teeth —that I began to fear the buzzards would come. Carrion, I very nearly was. They might have devoured me, still alive, as they did Gemar Quinto, after he had died. I was, however, visited by the final sensation, and I can swear that I felt not a sense of being crushed but of being hurled. I was hurled into space, like a dart.

A monstrous penetration, indeed. Still holding firm at the edge of a memory that resisted impoverishment, I confused, in a single plane, images I had experienced—the valley landscape, Jeronimo's cavern, Rosalia's face, the ebb and flow of a whole universe that had been palpable and solid—with images that today I find it hard to believe arose from me. When the former were spent, the latter remained. Crawling over the rocks, I no longer knew anything. Hunger itself had been overcome. My thirst had been extinguished. But what kept me going, as long as my body remained in oblivion—as dead as Roberto's body—was the motion of tall waves, their crests tossing me back and forth like a drowned man. If peace exists, that was peace, measureless and timeless.

Another reality began to emerge, ever so slowly, as if it had been embedded inside a husk of iron. I was swimming, armless, in that waterless channel, which was steaming like a cauldron. A silent, completely level tube, as infinite as distance. And not a single shadow present, absent all breathing, a reality without vibration but also without specters. There I was, maintaining myself on the surface, until I felt something heavy and cold upon my face like a frozen hand. The chill of its fingers, overcoming my exhaustion and immobility, obliged me to feel, to see, to hear, even to touch what was being born in me, in an extraordinarily concrete physical form. It was not the valley, I am certain. But, against the brooding landscape—always a kind of curtain of damp black plants—blending with the heavy smoke that kept rising, their faces transfigured by its chiaroscuro, the figures moving were the inhabitants of the valley. Jeronimo was not among them. Only those I had known in times gone by, those who had been and were no longer, Rosalia and her father, Roberto, and Gemar Quinto. They were waiting for me, leaning forward, as if at the railing of a pier. Suddenly I could hear their voices.

Strange dialogue that I can scarcely remember, it was monotonous and humorless, with now and then a brief pause, questions and replies that did not fit; but there was always the presence of the valley and the force of our past. I had just arrived, and it was difficult for me to understand why the woman spoke if I could still see her, under the ground, disfigured, putrefied, repugnant, inert; it was difficult to understand why, after coming out on the point of my knife, Roberto's eyes were once more gazing at me from his livid face; it was even more difficult to believe that Gemar Quinto, a mere skeleton on the floor of his cabin, could interrogate me. They had survived, every one of them, as if they were in the valley itself. Rosalia, however, was the first to say: "Close your fingers, Alexandre, and see what an ugly thing a hand is." And Roberto, right afterward, asking: "Alexandre, your hair?" Finally, Gemar Quinto: "The whole story, Alexandre, we shall not forget the whole story!" I knew that I was not the same as any one of these, who were like distant faces in the mist. Time, for me, had not yet been destroyed. The valley, on its physical crust, still subsisted, and Jeronimo was still a presence.

The vision was, however, most brief. So brief that, totally free of my own flesh, unquestionably beyond myself, I was able to concentrate upon the narrow zone that was my consciousness at its loneliest. A rigid slate, on which, initially, any projected light could be reflected. Initially, I repeat, because immediately thereafter it filled up with vague images—as if I were dreaming—tiny, lively, tremulous, like microbes swimming in a globule of blood. They twitched and turned as they moved. But in this confusion, what became clear was the effort to situate myself among them.

I truly was there, I finally understood. Everything that had gone before was concentrated there. On its surface, the valley's own earth. And what I had concluded—while I was fulfilling, in the valley, a destiny I had not sought but that had been imposed upon me like my body—now appeared to me with the force of something shameful: man, for himself, decides nothing. My experience would have been different if Rosalia had been my mother, if Jeronimo had been I, and I my father's father. Passively, however, we had become integrated in an immovable order, in a structure so vile that it did not even allow us our heart's own desire. A hundred years later—had I been able to choose—the valley would have been less harsh, would have had another name, and perhaps I would have had another body. Higher than myself, however, and with an abominable disregard for what should have become of me in my pure state, someone had made a determination. That slate, unappealable record, unimpeachable testimony, certainly did not belong to me. In my extreme immobility, imprisoned by my own blood, I lacked the courage to reject it. Consequently, it remained the sole active element, while above and below silence reigned, while the immeasurable void, colorless and formless, enveloped everything. Sensibility, absent. My heart, at a standstill.

Physically nothing, the roots of my body wholly lost, my existence—everything I was and had been—was limited to that energy which had not let itself be destroyed. Self-sufficient, resisting, released in an atmosphere that it could not itself identify, it found as its end objective the certainty that it had not been created for death. So that, irresistibly, it came to rest on top of those shapeless, denticulate rocks that recalled a crag in the process of formation.

A human body was sprawled on top of them. Its arms limp,

legs out straight, head turned upward, but with eyes closed. The hair of its head merged into its beard, still caked with mud. Its very blood, which traced a path upon the rocks, was now dried in the open wounds on its hand. A corpse, at first. But immediately afterward, as soon as breathing became deeper, feeling once more the warmth of my flesh, my pains returning, I perceived the cloudless sky. I thought of Jeronimo, and I heard his voice:

"The powers of fortune go with you!"

Had he been near me, even reclining on the floor of his cavern, Jeronimo would have jumped up and held me in his arms, as if protecting a part of himself. What I actually felt, when the blood resumed its flow in my veins, was more than the physical reencounter with myself. Much more, I assure you. Perhaps like being born an old man and, at the entryway to life, already bending under the knowledge of it and of all things. At the outset, however, I was not surprised by the fatigue that relaxed my body but rather by my deep breathing in the still air. Then, raising my injured hands, my temples pounding, I became aware of the foul odor of the rags I was wearing, the heavy flow of saliva in my mouth, my aching flesh. I closed my eyes in order not to see myself.

Then there appeared, bursting forth like something excessively objectified in its entirety and in its smallest details, the Ouro Valley. My ears picked up the sound of its wind, the voice of its inhabitants, the whinneying of its wild horses. The slough, with its putrescence. Its suffocating sultriness. The road, without beginning or end, laid out upon the dry red ground. Canuto's brickyard. Finally, Jeronimo's cavern. And last, a bit above Gemar Quinto's cabin, my own house, the kitchen, the pigsty.

Within me, driven by my awakened memory, the clouds were drawn aside. Alive, the valley, with all its monstrous vitality. I would have been able to identify it, every square foot. Had I bent close, I would have found on its ground the mark of my own feet. However, despite its all too visible and intimate physiognomy, something was transfiguring it—I was not sure whether it was the sight of it as a whole or the lack of Jeronimo's eyes, which had always seen it for me. Someone, not Jeronimo, standing with arms outstretched, was calling to me. Perhaps a woman, Rosalia. A tree, perhaps. However, when my hands closed, they closed upon a chip of stone. At last, I was able to get up.

I got up, unmistakably. My gaze cloudy, my loneliness stronger than my hunger, thirst, physical pain, I got up to walk, run if possible, flee that desolation which was expelling me as if in another birth. I dragged myself, unsupported, stumbling, to this day I know not for how many hours. In my mouth there was no longer any saliva. My throat was burning. In my chest, my heart, whether nearer life or nearer death I could not say. I crawled along, I repeat, as if I were something smashed by the now blood-colored sky. Seeing me, one would never have thought of a man—but would have feared to find, at the sight of my spectral shape, his own shadowy image, his final shadow, which appears when roots to the world are cut. But in my ears I could hear the sound of wings.

Their muffled echo, weak enough not to deform the silence, gave forth at last the figure of Gemar Quinto in complete outline. Amid black feathers, his skeleton had come apart. The arms, the rib cage, the skull that to me seemed more composed than his former face, full of splotches, swollen, repulsive. It stayed with me, as I crawled, for some time. When it disappeared, the mountain by then having been conquered, the next thing I saw was a panorama so violent that it awoke all that was still asleep within me. Then I felt the fever and, with the fever, I began to be able to see.

Down below, despite the distance and height at which I found myself, there came into precise view the vast green plateau. Forests, I thought to myself. The forests that Father had traversed and had made known to Jeronimo, that Jeronimo had spoken about, at home, when Rosalia was ill. In its depths lived another kind of humanity. My father, Abilio, had come from even farther away, from a city where the ocean turned into spray. But the clouds that were moving down below me flowed together in a heavy gray mass, cutting off my view. And the weak, sick man I was asked himself: "Should I go on walking?" Walk, ever more and more, without examining the way, walk until I found out that it would be impossible to return and impossible to see the Ouro Valley again with its wind, its people, its road. That black world could remain forgotten. Its attraction, extinguished. Further on, below the clouds, as a woodcutter, or a hunter like Gemar Quinto, I might perhaps acquire a new memory. With a different destiny would certainly come another identity. I must put out of my mind the figure of Jeronimo himself.

Now, in the depths of this night, I cannot tell you how I went ahead, descending, and how, with wounds all over my body, nearly naked, blood-smeared, I felt my way to that grove of trees. A bit more and hunger would have finished me. In my throat, live coals, and in my thirst, a flame. The fever, giving me chills, freezing my bones, was devouring me as if it were an invisible worm. With supreme effort, I embraced the tree trunk in order not to fall. Then, only a few feet away, I saw the shallow pool, the scummy water. I ran, stumbling all the way, until I laid my head in the mud and sucked the liquid as if I were sucking my mother's breast. Without strength for any other movement, I pulled a manioc plant out of the ground and, splitting its root, chewed, and slowly swallowed it.

What came after that, I never found out.

P A R T   F O U R

LISTEN, I BEG YOU. The sun will not be up for a while. Even running, Jeronimo will not arrive in time to prevent the past from fading out, unable now to take refuge in censure. Old Nathanael, less real perhaps, draws near. He no longer has his strange physiognomy, so simple and so serene, but it is his body that lies on the ground like a shadow and it is his shadow that stands up like a body. Listen, then. And forget about the ruins that surround me, the walls, the lantern, the howling wind itself. But hear me; perhaps as one who is again a human being, but who only a moment ago was rediscovering himself and, when faced with his own visage, repelled it like something outrageous. Let all eyes be averted. Leave the valley behind for a moment. And take a look. Before you do, answer me:

"Am I the one who lies there, sprawling, with his hands in the mud, dying of his wounds, so much alone in the silence and in the world?"

I am, indeed. Away from the valley, still far from myself, I had once more lost the warmth of my blood and once more what may have been life was absent. I do not know if I was entirely dead. I cannot even say if my flesh had not begun to rot, if my blood had not already begun to dry up. Come closer, a bit closer, and don't be afraid. Perchance you will smell the bad odor. Probably you will not recognize, in the disfigured face, the countenance of the man who is here, the lantern light fixing the harsh outlines. Come closer, I insist.

But don't make any noise. Come in silence, with soft steps, as if keeping vigil over the dead body of a brother or a friend. Ask no questions. Let all action be concentrated in a moment of expectancy, all thoughts be reduced to this question: "What will happen?" Let human curiosity be curbed because, while the stagnant water was stimulating the movement of my lips, reality was slowly coming back. At first, merely nausea. And, before the onset of anguish, the vague outline of a powerful face. Jeronimo was in the circle of my open eyes.

An inexistent source of help, perhaps. As inexistent as the voice of my father, Abilio. Had this not been true, I would not have raised to a sitting position, only to succumb to a despair I had never known till then. I was the prisoner of abandon, uncertainty, and for the first time, fear. The great fear of a universe that had proved to be indifferent—mute trees, the cloudless sky. The fear that grew, mounting always, to the point of not allowing me to discover my identity before I began to contemplate nature all around me. Finally, you may be sure, all of you who hear me, someone spoke for me, into my own ear: "Your name is Alexandre. Can you hear all right? Alexandre, who came from the valley."

Understand me, now. I came from the valley, Alexandre was my name. But do not interrupt, and listen. Listen, I implore you.

With the premonition that no understanding would be possible between that world and myself, with all my irrational barriers up, I violently coaxed my memory. It had saved me once and it could save me again. With extreme effort, it might be able to revive the Ouro Valley, restoring the inner order that it once had. Mental anarchy, however, prevailed. And what characterized it was not the fear, not the lack of control, not even the frustration of instinct, but an anxiety that made me appear to myself like some imaginary being.

No doubt my physical constitution had changed. Though unacceptable, an illogical plan was demanded by the circumstances. To counter it, I restrained myself, my face buried in my hands. I could hear myself saying in my natural voice, but saying very softly: "I no longer am the same." Between the two, the one who had said good-by to Jeronimo at the edge of the valley and the one who was now awakening, there was more than an interval of time. There was death, I knew. I had been buried and had not totally escaped oblivion. Throbbing before me even the valley seemed unreal. Jeronimo himself, now so distant, no longer owned a distinguishable form. The rest were entirely forgotten: Rosalia, my wife; Gemar Quinto, the leper; Canuto, the potter. As if a supernatural arm were holding me aloft, I was conscious of the air, the clouds like a shroud about my body.

Gone was all brightness. A powder blast, in my ear, would not have gotten my attention. But, seeming to arise out of nowhere, breaching my muteness, racking the flesh in that torture which was the pulsation of life, my heart beat, thump by thump, under my still rigid hand. Then I screamed like a madman. Whether directed at the earth, the wind, the trees, my scream resounded inarticulately. And its echo, lingering, served to convert me into what I after all had never ceased being—a man, a creature integrated in the common condition.

I got up, with difficulty, and began again to walk. I was astonished at the plants, the bushes, the rocks. My feet were bare and bruised. My body was almost naked. My hair, long and bushy. My beard, fouled with mud, protected my face against the cold. I would stop, now and again, to breathe the difficult air, my lungs in pain. I was alive, no doubt about it. I had truly come back to life. And, though I was incapable of more ample reasoning, my brain was now working constantly. Fortified by my memory, which linked me hopelessly to the Ouro Valley, it was operating like a piece of defective machinery: "I am walking." Then in a moment: "I am walking without Jeronimo." Next: "Where am I walking?" And the reply: "I know I am walking." I kept traveling, in confusion, my gaze now sharper and registering, as day began to break, distant peaks and green foliage. The outer noises—birds singing, wind in the leaves, water in the streams—were now becoming recognizable and filled my still somewhat deaf ears. I was rediscovering the world and a truth.

Unexpectedly, a kind of joy—which I had never known, not even as a child, in the valley—took possession of every part of me. I may have laughed. Suddenly my heart beat faster. My step grew firmer. And, had not night intervened, I might have run. The stars did not frighten me. The darkness caused me no emotion. I lay down, on the ground, and closed my eyes.

When I opened them, it was light. Still weak, incapable of warming, it was nonetheless sunlight. I tried to glimpse the sky, get my bearings, but my thoughts immediately turned to Abilio, my father. How I managed to recede, so freely, to the point of recalling my father without Jeronimo's assistance, I do not know. I can tell you that, precisely then, my thought became quite clear: "I am on my way to find Abilio's world." And even more clearly: "I come perhaps to carry on his destiny." He had gone to the valley, a fugitive. And I, a fugitive, was coming from the valley. What I would find, later on, or tomorrow, I could not foretell.

The region was, however, quite different. The earth was dark, the trees enormous, the wind almost absent, and water plentiful. Pools, streams, creeks. My route, a path, was indicated less by the marks of human feet than by the slippery mud. Heavy clouds, ever moving, would hide the sun from moment to moment. The high humidity penetrated everything. Luxuriantly, the vegetation kept intertwining. Cited by Jeronimo, Abilio came to mind, speaking of wild boars, monkeys, and tapirs. Afterward, and as long as I walked, I got acquainted with the rain, heavy downpours falling at frequent intervals.

Drained of strength, the water aggravating the wounds I had suffered on my body—especially on my hands and feet—virtually skating on mud, thus it was that I found the first house. I don't know if that hovel can be called a house. Call it home, for someone was living in it. The first man I had seen since I left Jeronimo. Like me, he had long hair, a beard down to his chest, bare feet; his clothes were no more than a deerskin vest and short denim pants, held up at the waist by a piece of vine, which substituted for his belt. Seeing me come up, he drew near. Quite an event in his life, one could see. He approached, with eyes full of curiosity, examining me. To me he seemed a fantastic creature.

He took me by the hand, silently, and led me to his hut. That tree, to have such a trunk, must have been centuries old. Using fire, no doubt taking advantage of a dry spell, and as if building a canoe, he had hollowed out a large space. Evidently he had had an axe as he had made supports, which he set in the ground, and erected a roof pole, which he then covered with palm thatch. Half on the ground, half in the tree trunk, his hut was not lacking in ingenuity. When I entered, I could see that he slept in the trunk. There he kept his oxhide. There, in a corner, his long knife. A bit later I learned how he protected himself when he slept. He partitioned his shelter in the tree trunk from the unprotected room with a wide sort of plank, extending quite high, whose upper part was pierced with small holes. The air he breathed passed through them. Outside, while he slept, wood in the stone fireplace blazed all night long. After having me lie down, on his oxhide, he broke the silence. He was sitting on his haunches and had a sharp look, when he asked:

"What is your name?"

"Alexandre," I replied.

"All right," he added, "my name is Terto."

He got up, heaped wood in the fireplace, and lit it. In a clay pot he put water on to boil. He showed not the slightest haste and seemed unaware of time. Later, calling me, he bathed my wounds with warm water. He went to the oxhide, which he lifted up, and got out an undershirt and the pants he gave me to wear. Making me lie down again, Terto left. He was not long in coming back, with some leaves. He prepared a sort of tea and served me in a drinking cup, also of clay. His hand open in a gesture of leave-taking, he said:

"I have to run the traps. I won't be long."

Left to myself, my muscles at ease, still a bit dazed, I was overcome by fatigue. For an instant, above the darkness created when my eyelids closed, there rose the image of Jeronimo. I don't know if he was in the valley, for I did not even notice what he was doing. But Jeronimo's teeth were clenched and his bull neck was so strong it looked like a pillar.

I waked up, without Terto's having returned. Feeling more tranquil, I waited for him. A few minutes later, he arrived. On his back he was carrying a dead animal—a paca, if I am not mistaken. He was on his way to the creek to bathe, he said, and would be right back to prepare our meal. As soon as he returned, I could see that we were already into night. A miraculous man, this Terto. Without asking my assistance, thinking me perhaps seriously ill, he got the game ready, roasting a part and preparing the rest to be hung up to dry. He served me my portion and, after piling on wood to make a little bonfire, sat down to eat. He seemed at that moment not to be concerned about anything at all.

"So your name is Alexandre?" he asked, chewing.

Fearing lest he ask where I came from, why I had come to that remote wilderness, I decided to make his curiosity mine. I was above all concerned whether he knew of the Ouro Valley's existence. How would he react, should he already know about the valley? What would he do, should he take me for a fugitive? Before he could ask me, then, I asked him:

"And why do you, Terto, live here? How did you get here? Have you always lived this way, all alone?"

Terto looked at me, very calmly, without concern. He tossed the bone away, settled himself more comfortably, and began speaking. I listened, a bit restless, as I had always listened to Jeronimo.

"Two or three years ago"—his voice melted into the night sounds that come from the forest, as in a musical background— "these lands belonged to the government. Completely uninhabited—I actually think that even the Indians have never lived here. The tax collector, down in the village of Coaraci, explained to the people that it was sufficient to have the land boundaries registered, in Ilheus, for them to become owners. Many registered their claims. Almost all, however, lost their ownership. Land was given but people had to fell the trees, burn and clear the brush, plant grass or cacao. As far as I know, two of us stayed on. Myself, Terto, and Paizinho, who had been a hired gunman.

"There the land is, still unoccupied. At the time of the leprosy outbreak, and that has been some time, the lepers who were forced to leave opened up some trails. They came through here, these lepers, and I don't know what became of them. I arrived a long time afterward, all because of my grandfather. Timoteo, my grandfather. A very stingy man, my grandfather. Back in the village, in Coaraci, everyone remembers him.

"The old fellow had lung trouble, some strange kind of asthma. In the wet season he would wheeze like a puffing adder. He is the one who raised me. He lived at the entrance to the village, on the river bank. The three of us lived there, he, my grandmother, and I. A mass of wrinkles, dressed to her dying day in her shapeless blue denim shift, Grandma Zefa felt for her husband the kind of respect a slave must feel. She did the cooking, the washing, and every night fixed the watercress soup that the old man drank. Their daughter, my mother, died in childbirth. My father, who came from Sergipe, left for parts unknown with nothing but the clothes on his back. And I stayed behind, reared by the old folks, in that propped-up house, with its packed dirt floor, as leaky as a sieve when it rained. There were neither benches nor table. We ate sitting on the ground, from clay dishes. We slept on mats, smelling the dust of the earth.

"Grandpa Timoteo, however, was one of the richest men in the village. The richest, to be exact. He had a fair-sized ranch, his cattle, four houses. In his room, ever within reach of his hands and eyes, a padlocked metal trunk. Inside was his money. Talk about spending, he hardly spent anything. Often, turning on his wife, he would explode with shouts and curses because she had not saved a piece of brown sugar or had used up too soon her supply of salt and kerosene. Every night, with his little lamp on the floor, he would count and recount his money. I wonder if anyone in this world ever loved anything the way the old man loved his money. He lived for his money, my grandfather did.

"He beat me almost to death, once, because I touched the trunk. On another occasion he threatened to drive my grandmother out of the house because she let a drought refugee keep a wicker basket in the living room. But when I felt able to work, I left the old man. However, I stayed on in the village. I hired out as an apprentice at seu* Rodolfo's blacksmith shop. Plenty of hard work, tending the fire, hammering the iron. On Sundays I used to go visit the old man. Each week I found him more decrepit. His asthma was getting worse and he choked when he coughed. He was sweating through every pore. He quit shaving

* Colloquial form of Senhor; when followed by a proper name, it implies respect on the part of the speaker.

and his hair turned whiter than cotton. So thin and stooped he was that they said he had a knot in his spine. He seems to have foreseen death because, before he lay down never to rise again, he took it into his head to get rid of everything he possessed. He sold the ranch, the cattle, the houses. I learned later that he had commercial houses change all his coins into paper money. So many bills must have really stuffed the trunk. When he became bedridden, mere skin and bones, I don't know whether his mind was more on his money or on life itself. One day, badly weakened, barely able to open his mouth to eat, he called his wife.

" 'Bring me the trunk,' he said.

"He had the key to the padlock in his clenched hand. He was drooling and smelled of urine. The old woman was in tears. I was present and it was after midday. The sun was shining and the light came in through chinks in the plaster. The neighbors, who hated him, were not aware of anything. On the mat, breathing noisily, he opened the trunk with the greatest of difficulty. We stood watching, the old woman and I. He would not be long in dying, perhaps a matter of minutes. He put his hands, pale and trembling, into the trunk, and gathered the banknotes into a single pile. His eyes, wide open, were still shining.

"He asked for his lamp, for them to light it and bring it to him. His wife, the same listless relic, went out and came back with the lighted lamp. She set the lamp on the floor, beside the trunk. Sitting upright, with an enormous effort, clenching the banknotes in hands that were more like claws, he touched them to the flame. His wife turned away. The money blazed and burned. And when he fell, his chest heaving the more because of his emotion, I noticed that his fingers were burned. He still had his fingertips in the ashes. When I reached him, he was no longer breathing.

"My grandmother, a few days later, also passed on. What remained, as my inheritance, was the house in which I was raised, merely the house, as its furnishings were worthless. And, having lived alone up to that time, and what with the tax collector's advising people to register their claims, I went to Ilheus and registered my piece of land. Paizinho went with me, I remember, but there he went his own way.

"At first, I missed the village very much. Seu Rodolfo's anvil would even have been preferable. We, however, do not choose our future. I kept staying on, felled trees on an acre or so, cleared a firebreak, and touched off the blaze. Today, the grass is growing fine. Had you come two days later, you would not have found me here. I need to put on the knapsack and head for Coaraci. I'm going to get some things I need. If possible, I'll bring a cow, a bull, some heifers."

He had talked a lot and hadn't gotten tired. He was watching me, now, as the fire illuminated his still youthful face. He was an owner of land and was helping to improve the world by the strength of his arms. He had indeed known human egotism— his grandfather had taught him a great lesson. But, had he been born in the valley, and come from the valley, would he be the same? Would he not, like me, feel at a loss to do anything, a tremendous despair? He was watching me, his gaze attentive, I was well aware. And he did not hesitate to say, straight out, what he was thinking:

"You're not like us," he said, laughing.

"Why?" I asked.

"I don't know," he replied, "but I think you came into this world only yesterday."

Then he asked, getting up:

"And how were you injured in this way?"

He let his own intent gaze meet mine. Expectantly, he was forcing me to keep up with him, mentally to follow his reasoning. He was like a child, clapping his hands and exclaiming:

"You can't answer, you see!"

Perhaps he thought I was one of those hunters, descended from Indians, like Gemar Quinto. Someone, perhaps, who had lost his way. At best, someone from a village more distant than his own. Anything except what, in truth, I might well have been. Convinced that he was wrong, I felt the need to be protective, and in relation to him I acted as if I were Jeronimo in relation to myself. Here was Jeronimo, present still another time. Getting to my feet, the two of us beside the campfire but separated like the children of two different worlds, I asked with a shout:

"Have you ever heard talk, around here, of a place called the Ouro Valley?"

The valley as a whole—all its barrenness, the cactus, the mud of the slough, Jeronimo and the wild horses, my house, the heat, the road, Canuto, the cavern, the shifting wind—the liquid image of it, like tears, made my eyes sting. The burning embers, the flames moving like tongues, did not warm my skin. Opposite me, surprised and apprehensive, Terto was waiting. I repeated the question, again shouting, no longer hearing the forest noises in the night. He, however, did not flinch. He pinned my arms, with hands hardened by farm chores, his expression almost childlike, disarming, innocent. He looked at me, with no sign of fear, and said:

"You're delirious, fellow, and you've a fever!"

I shouted even louder, my voice seeming strange to me:

"I'm not delirious!"

Terto pleaded:

"You're burning up. Lie down. Rest a little longer."

And he added, lowering his voice:

"We're alone in this forest. Miles and miles separate us from Paizinho. From here to the village is eight days' journey. Either we control our nerves or the forest will drive us mad."

I sat down at the very moment it started to rain. I rested my face on my arms, the heat that rose from the flames sustaining me like food. Without making the slightest movement, staying on his feet, Terto once again was waiting. He was of course hoping that my hallucination would go away, that my blood would subside, that the forest would not destroy my mind. After a while, he sat down beside me and said:

"In the village, Alexandre, you'll get better."

He continued, as if wishing to convince me:

"There are men and women, in the village. In time, you will get well. You can also register your land claim. It's all a matter of time, Alexandre."

To forget, impossible. The road was getting stronger. In bold relief, Rosalia's face was coming back. With their forefeet in the air, their manes flying, the wild horses were fighting and leaping. The elder Luna, with his mouth agape, his hands bloody. Gemar Quinto, his body hidden in a clay-colored sheet, dragging himself through the dust. And Jeronimo, with his fat cheeks, a giant. It was the valley, the Ouro Valley, its crusty earth and its leaden sky. Eternal and ever restless, its wind. And the sound of the rain that came from outside like one more form of torture, finally became indistinguishable from a softer sound. The wings, in blind flight, black in the darkness, over the skeleton of the leper.

I extended my arms, lifted my head, opened my eyes. Terto, with arms crossed, continued to wait. The need to explain was greater than self-control and broke loose like an explosion, tearing through my heart until it came to stop on my wavering lips. A last-minute reproof held it back, and my mental state grew confused: "Should I repeat?" With my hands, I steadied myself on the oxhide. So bright was the firelight that it seemed to me like a sun. The rain was not letting up, outside. Then, I said:

"I come from the Ouro Valley."

"But there is no such place," Terto assured me, "and you could not have come from a place that does not exist."

He lowered his voice, with compassion, and, to convince me, said:

"It's all a bad dream, Alexandre."

But he did ask me to say what the valley was like, who lived in the valley, where it was, and why I had left it only to be found sick and covered with wounds. He insisted, above all, on the question:

"Where is the valley?"

"I don't know," I answered.

"If you don't know"—Terto was speaking forcefully now—"it's because it's nothing more than a delusion. A delusion caused by the forest. The forest devours men's souls. It creates nightmares and, often, men are returned to their villages like cane pulp drained of its juice."

He concluded, as I listened in silence:

"In the village you will know many of these men."

He raised the large plank, closing off the opening in the tree trunk, leaned on me, and said:

"Let's get some sleep, it's late."

Terto was, I repeat, a miraculous man. The following day, always preferring that I not help him, he sharpened his knife, ran his traps to get fresh game, prepared a large amount of meat for drying, wrapped in papaya leaves the two loaves of brown sugar that were left, fitted a new handle to his axe, and, thus, in innumerable tasks, busied himself until night. He went almost without speaking, during the day. When he lay down to sleep, he advised me:

"Tomorrow, very early, we will travel."

I never thought the village of Coaraci would be so far away. I had not believed the forests would be so immense, the trees so tall, the rain so incessant, with only a miraculous man like Terto able to keep his bearings in those gloomy depths, where huge roots ran over the ground, danger lurked at every step, and insects and mosquitoes swarmed like bees around a hive.

In the densely foliated treetops, clumps of tree orchids would have fallen but for the support of nets of twisted vines. We would see snakes, now and again, crossing paths and trails. Imperceptible to the eye, far away, the sky remained in hiding. Great birds would fly up. With his knife, skilled in that kind of work, Terto cut a passageway; alert, cautious, he kept advancing, slowly and surely. He had quit talking and, since the journey began, had not yet uttered a word.

I was carrying the axe, the oxhide, and the knapsack. Terto, with another leather sack on his back, was bringing the provisions. We kept walking in this way, without haste, the entire day. The main punishment came from the rain, rarely in heavy downpours but unendingly in a fine mist, exasperating, penetrating, and finally, by afternoon, chilly. Terto did not feel it, as he went steadily ahead. When night began to fall and after he had selected the safest place, he cut some palm fronds. He set up a kind of lean-to, and it was not at all easy for him, after finding dry twigs, to make a fire. Finally, we ate. I slept half the night with Terto standing watch. The other half, he slept and I stood guard.

In the jungle, after a certain time, the monotony grows. Everything is the same. If it weren't for the dangers, perhaps the senses would be brutalized and dulled. It's easy to lose self-control, to get lost, not to know forward from backward. By myself, I probably could not have gotten out of the forest. But with his canine sense of smell, seldom stopping for bearings, Terto took me to the outskirts of Coaraci.

"We'll be there in a few hours," he had alerted me.

A moment later, a clear view opened, and we could then see the pastures, the short grass, a few head of cattle. Visible on the ground, skirting the fences, the path that human feet had kept clear. We were arriving, soaked and worn out. One small hill to cross, according to Terto, and then we would catch sight of the village. Women, who were washing clothes in the river, had probably caught sight of us. And they would run swiftly to the village to announce that two men were coming back from the forest.

There at last was the little village. It was strung out on a slope, the rude houses joined one to another, and, at a distance it recalled some misshapen lizard. Built on the highest piece of ground, perhaps to escape the flooding river, it might rather have been called a temporary encampment. Under the heavy overcast, silent and apparently uninhabited, the village seemed to recede as we advanced. Finally, we began to ascend the slope.

"We're home," said Terto.

Leaning against the wall or sitting in the doorway of their houses, the women as well as the men barefooted, everyone came up to shake Terto's and my hand when they saw us arrive. He introduced me to one after another, continuing to walk until he stopped at the door of the house that had belonged to his grandfather. He pushed the door, which gave and swung open. No sooner had we entered and Terto thrown open the window to a sudden jet of sunlight than we saw someone move, in the corner of the room, on the mat. Bending down, after putting his knapsack on the floor, Terto recognized the intruder because he inquired in a normal tone:

"Is that you, Erlindo?"

A creature of perhaps my own age or Terto's, he revealed his shattered inner world through his eyes and their childish fright. Cowering, as if afraid of a beating, he did not in turn recognize the master of the house. He jumped up suddenly and, at a run, escaped by the back door. Terto explained:

"The forest, the forest inflicted this misery upon Erlindo."

And he concluded, in an outburst:

"Alexandre, the village is full of men like that!"

Weary, we did nothing more. Terto lay down, on the mat where Erlindo had been, and went right to sleep, still with muddy feet, but at peace. I also lay down, incapable of a single thought. On my body, the wounds were healing.

The village revealed itself, day after day, while Terto was offering his house in exchange for tools, a yoke of oxen, groceries. On an incline, upright though out of plumb, the two facing rows of houses hid behind sparse trees with exposed roots. Men, women, dogs, pigs, cows, calves, passed by, climbing or descending, clumsily, in the mud. Occasionally some man would go by singing, with sad voice, often to be interrupted by the shouts of children. And the rainstorms, constantly, washing everything off.

The villagers' curiosity rose up around me, the stranger who had arrived with Terto. Terto remembered Erlindo, Erlindo and so many others who, deep in the forest, had transformed their dreams of riches into nightmares. Though less so than Erlindo,

I too was the victim of an hallucination. Evidently, I did not know where I came from. The Ouro Valley, moreover, was a mirage. The painful mirage created by the forest. People could accept many things, of course. There was the ocean, to be sure. A city like Ilheus did exist, in truth. But, who could believe in an arid valley, eternally scourged by the wind, inhabited by brutish men and wild horses? Who could admit a rocky plain, without life or vegetation, on top of a vast mountain? Who could accept a region where crime is permitted, the sky is black, the heat suffocates, and man's heart no longer pulses like a human heart? Pitiful the image of such insanity, sick the mind that could conceive of such a universe. Where it actually was, I did not know. Meanwhile, I mentioned names, described the types of humanity that people that land, harsh as rock. I did not in the least forget the muddy slough.

Nowhere in the village, from one house to another, had anyone ever heard of the Ouro Valley. Residing there were men from the outside who had traveled all roads, hunters and gatherers of the forest, wood cutters, the descendants of Indians, but no one had ever met a single person who had heard from anyone else any reference to the valley. It was a delusion, shattering and violent, but still a delusion. The forest had destroyed the health of my mind.

Terto continued all his efforts to help me. Identified with the village, acquainted with everyone, he tried in vain to incorporate me into the group. I was not interested in its problems or in its concerns. I kept to my house, aloof, mute, like a prisoner, like a stranger unversed in the language and the customs. I worked hard, meanwhile, to settle, to remain, to become integrated. Innumerable times I leaned against trees, listening to the men, observing the women. Their glances, however, were suspicious, prudent, and kept me at a distance. Perhaps, in the minds of the villagers, I was suffering from an incurable malady. Somebody whom the forest had ruined for the rest of his days. Something useless, no doubt, like Erlindo himself. I found out, days afterward, that one person did not share that opinion. It was Rodolfo, the blacksmith.

The matter of the house settled, the implements acquired, the necessary oxen obtained, Terto made haste to return to his landholdings. He opposed the idea of my returning to the forest, my state might be aggravated, I ought to stay in the village. I should use good judgment, and, furthermore, the opportunity had arisen:

"Rodolfo wants to try you out, at his shop," he said. "The work is hard but it will keep your mind off things."

Terto left, to plunge into the forest. I stayed behind, sleeping at the shop, feeling good with the fire constantly burning. Those flames brought Jeronimo's cavern back to life, and in a sense they put Jeronimo back at my side. During work, the heat of the coals on my face, I would let my gaze fasten upon the fire and the valley would always emerge, infinitesimal, from the flames. No matter that my hands were full and I could hear the blows of Rodolfo's hammer. What fascinated me was the valley, Rosalia in her bed, Gemar Quinto crawling, the scorched earth, Jeronimo especially. An unparalleled energy flowed to aid my nerves at those moments. It transported me, unquestionably, to the valley. I would forget Rodolfo, the village would disappear, and there was an absolute suppression of all immediate reality. My mental reaction was linked to the past, was one with the valley that the village judged to be imaginary. Holding its shape, it would slowly fade until there was only Jeronimo's face, beautiful in its rough way, finally giving way to a rebirth of the flames.

Communication with the village, after that, became more difficult. Too close by, never varying his daily contact, Rodolfo some days irritated me. With scars from burns on arms and hands, a thin face, rust under his fingernails, a piece of burlap around his waist like an apron, he was coarser-looking than anyone imaginable. Nor was there anyone like him for mastery of fire and iron. At first, he used to watch me in silence. Then he had started screaming his orders. Finally, at the height of his fury, he would burst out:

"You are an ass, a stupid ass."

I should have gotten out, as Terto had done, and, since my adaptation was hopeless, since my integration into the village was frustrated, I should have left as soon as possible, heading down the road, futureless, alone with my past. This very man, however, who thought himself stronger than the iron he wrought, had awakened in me the example of Jeronimo. The dead man, who had so long been buried within himself, and had slowly come back to life, finally found the opportunity to gain complete possession of himself. That opportunity arose one afternoon, and the man who created it was Rodolfo, the blacksmith.

Coming from the back—where he lived in a room that had been built, inside the shop, to serve as kitchen—irritated and in what might be called a feverish state, the blacksmith was beside himself with fury the moment he saw me. With my head lowered, I could see his big feet. His upraised arms were swinging about, as the insult was hurled from compressed lips:

"You lazy swine, you stupid swine!"

My eyes, which I had averted, discovered the fire, crackling, bright, powerful. As if the valley wind were whistling in my ears and I were in the valley itself marching down the highroad,

I felt Jeronimo's hands, heavy and aggressive, upon my shoulders. From Jeronimo came the sudden outburst, the inescapable order: "Throw this dog in the fire!" Jeronimo's cheeks inflated, his bull neck turned as he concluded: "And be quick!" I lifted my eyes, the muscles of my face unmoving, and suddenly met the blacksmith's startled eyes. But I grabbed him by the arms, the wind ceaselessly blowing, Jeronimo filling all the space, and I pushed him back against a pile of scrap iron. He broke his fall with his hands, which started to bleed. At that instant, as if Jeronimo were seeing for me, I picked up a piece of iron that was being forged. The bloody redness of the weapon, incandescent in my hand, brought Roberto back to mind. And I screamed:

"I'll burn your eyes out, you son of a bitch!"

Outside, by chance, it was not raining. Whether passing by, or responding to the commotion, someone came in by the open door. The blacksmith quickly cried out, and, in less than a second, there were lots of people running to his aid. With the red-hot iron still in my hand, and Jeronimo helping me, I reached the door to the back of the house, leaped through the opening, and walking as if I knew where I was going, headed for the forest. They didn't follow me, didn't try to catch me—they must have thought the forest would in time eliminate their victim. They let me go, watching me from a distance, as they would a condemned man. I was escaping from the village only to sink deeper into my fantastic delirium. I could go, without protection, food, or resource. The forest, for them, was ever a monster without pity. I would be devoured, indeed, devoured as a fly by a giant spider. But when I had gotten past the clearings, and I once more plunged into the forest, I thought of Terto. He would still be traveling, alert and wary. How he was able to drive the yoke of oxen, I did not know. To find him again would be impossible. I could never locate his tracks, and it would be unbearable to hear him deny the existence of the valley, to hear him defend the village of Coaraci. Much better the solitude, the endless march, the journey without a course. Beyond the Ouro Valley—Jeronimo had asserted, invariably citing my father Abilio—the world was vast, as vast as the immense sky. It had infinite forests but it also had abundant cities. As many villages as there were cactuses in the valley. Should I walk and keep on going, some person would be waiting for me and some house would shelter me. Men and stones, Jeronimo used to say, were always to be found in this world.

I looked hard, by then enveloped by the thick foliage, with night falling in deep shadows, I looked hard for anything that might suggest a human foot, a grown-over path, the tiniest trail. The track of a stray, something that could lead me somewhere. But, as if they were fast moving clouds, the shadows suddenly merged, horrifying and impenetrable. To attempt to advance would mean tearing my flesh on the spiny undergrowth. No way to distinguish North from South. I could not make a fire, I had forgotten my knife, and, except for my arms, all I had left was the piece of iron, now cold like the damp bushes. Jeronimo once again came to my aid, or Abilio, but my lips found these words:

"Be weak and you die on the gallows."

With the piece of iron, I cleared an area on the ground the size of a chair bottom. I sat down, the piece of iron in my hand, and thought, without discouragement, about what Jeronimo had heard from Gemar Quinto: "The forest animals detect human flesh by its smell." And the hunger I was beginning to feel kept growing. My saliva thickened. My eyelids grew heavier, sleep was sapping all my strength. But I resisted. I resisted in a way that only Jeronimo would have chosen, by biting my lips to cause physical pain, forcing my mind awake with a mute question: "Have I left, in the village, the last things I am to own in this world?" Ephemeral question, virtually lost upon one who could not answer it. Vigilant, my senses responded, alert, ready, active. An animal—it could have been nothing else—was approaching. My nostrils flared, my ears picked up the faintest sounds, once more I caught my breath. Crouching, as if to jump, I waited. My eyes were watching, their own light aglow. I stayed motionless, with clenched teeth, for a time.

One could discern, amid the nighttime noises that filled the forest, paws crushing damp leaves. Soft, stealthy, the footfalls seemed guided by a logic. They kept coming closer, firmly, more precise, more perceptible, very near. In the shadows, all my muscles went rigid; my open eyes were fixed upon two embers that hovered in the air as they probed. The distance, perhaps two yards, was short. Like clams, my hands gripped the iron bar. One animal confronting another, we looked at each other as if testing which was the weaker and which might die. I thrust out my chest, my eyes burning, my knees brushing the ground, and I yelled loud and stridently—a frightening yell, unexpected, so violent and brutal that the animal jumped back, in fear. I got up, as it ran away, and yelled again without really knowing what I was doing.

A tremendous lassitude then came. I didn't feel tired but I was panting. My hands were sweaty, as were my forehead and chest. Sittting down again, with night advancing and turning colder, I had a strange sense of security not felt since I separated from Jeronimo. Tranquil and protective the trees seemed to me. Alert as always, my senses functioning like swift tenacles, I saw

a tableau that perhaps the shadows had made reappear and that, though already much darkened by time, was nonetheless complete.

Jeronimo took my hand—the tiny hand of that child of four— in the dark of night, and, setting me on his shoulder, at the mouth of the cavern, pointed with his arm toward the sleeping valley. Made of lead, the sky was black. The shadows were just beginning to gather on the hot plateau. He exclaimed seriously, as if the child were an adult:

"All that blackness could be made white!"

Then it was that, putting me down on the ground, he went inside the cavern and returned with a leather pail full of goat's milk. He called to me by name:

"Alexandre."

And he said:

"Watch!"

With his arms held very high, he poured into space, in a circle of white tears, all the milk he had brought. It was short, rapid, but rather beautiful. That is the way Jeronimo used to entertain me, when I was a child. Jeronimo, my old friend, Jeronimo, who now, in his cavern, could not see the shadows that were enveloping me, could not accompany me on my uncertain journey.

I understood, at a time when I no longer believed I would escape from the constantly repeated and unchanging forest, less exhausted now because I had made use of Terto's lessons—how to improvise a safe shelter, how to find an old trail, what fruits one should eat—I understood that the world would be unthinkable without colors and hues. The forest does not belong to the world. The permanent, irreplaceable green that dominates everything wearies one at first. Then it irritates. Finally, it tortures.

I closed my eyes in order not to see it, in the leaves, in the grass, in the rushes along streams. It hurt my eyes, bluntly contradicted the open coloring of the Ouro Valley. The green of the forest is less a color than a nightmare. It infects the earth that it hides, triumphs over the water that reflects it passively. But, walking aimlessly, I was on the lookout for a trail, a narrow path, anything that might suggest the cut of a machete.

"In the forest there is always someone's trail," Terto had advised me.

And Terto had saved me. On the edge of a swamp, terrifying in the greenness of its water, I noticed that, among the wild banana plants, some were putting out shoots, in a straight row. I ran, pell-mell, and bent down. I examined them, carefully, like a scientist. There it was, close to the ground, the cut. Someone had cut them down. One name came to my lips: "Paizinho?" And the question that followed cheered me for a moment: "Was I perhaps once more in Terto's country?" I proceeded, in anguish, one foot and then the other, over that route. One more afternoon, the following day, and, finally, signs of a campfire long since extinguished. Not far away someone must be living—or could it be another village? The dirt gradually let itself be seen, the path took shape, and now it was a road. Trees were getting sparser, clumps of thorn bushes were disappearing. I could now contemplate the gray clouds with fascination. Blackish, the earth. And, in a manner unforeseen by the dirty, ragged man with shaggy hair and beard, a deeper awareness almost paralyzed him: the unvarying panorama ended and the landscape that now began was a frontier. Across the black land, the soft green was shading into a violent yellow. It was a grove of low trees, all of a kind, with a carpet of dry leaves covering the roots, and their yellow fruit provoked my hunger. I broke open the first one, on a rock, sucking the almond-like seeds. A taste as of honey. I had come back into the world, I could tell, because there were varieties of color. The water, which came down in the creeks, had a bluish tinge.

Jeronimo, always drawing upon Abilio, used to refer to the cacao groves. A well-watered country, without swamps, but humid. And now I was arriving there, remaking, perhaps in the opposite direction, my father's trip, to a world that did not seem to me unreal because Jeronimo had prepared me. Before long I would be coming upon a house, farther on perhaps, but perched on the bank of a stream. I must keep walking, and fast, before the gray clouds should thicken and become showers. A singular desire was impelling me—the strange wish to banish solitude forever. I was dying to talk, to see around me creatures like myself, to hear voices, to hear laughter.

Perhaps—and who can say?—to forget the Ouro Valley, its harsh crust, its furnacelike heat, its unsociable inhabitants, its eternal wind. Would that I might amputate, as if it were an arm, my obsession with the gallows, its now dried wood, its hardened rope. Be done with my entire past, the least shadow, Rosalia with her temperament, Roberto without his eyes, the untamed horses, Gemar Quinto, and the road. But what about Jeronimo? Would not the valley always subsist, on top of my own grave, as long as there was a Jeronimo? Could I, at one extreme of my entire being, could I eliminate Jeronimo? If I did, wouldn't it be like eliminating myself? And who would recall the valley the most, who, if not Jeronimo himself? I was almost running, the rain coming down noisily, and at that moment there was no reasoning or nobility of spirit, governed as I was by my instincts, like a hunting dog. I was intoxicated by the smell of moist earth, the resin of cacao trees, the unfounded presentiment that, the very next day, I would eat cooked meat and sleep on a mat. One more effort, a final effort, and I would seek shelter with these hands, at any door, for my exhausted body.

It was night, pitch-dark, when I knocked with my open hands on the first door. It was raining, but there was no wind. I beat on the door, hard, as if commanding. From inside came a voice and from inside a light flowed out, in a trickle, underneath the door. I heard the sound of the door latch abruptly raised. And when the door opened my bloodshot eyes registered a scene that I was never able to forget. I can see it now, concrete, real, as at that moment.

With the lamp in his hand, his white hair disheveled, a tall, very tall man stood looking at me without fear. An old man of ruddy complexion who, I could see the moment he took a step, limped with one leg. At his side, covered by a canvas cloak, a fat woman with eyes not yet awake. Further back, inside the room, a boyish youth, still beardless, kept looking at me as if he were seeing a ghost. Finally, close beside the boy, a young girl, redheaded and freckled, but calm and completely unconcerned. All our shadows were being projected on the walls. The old man's hand shook, one could see from the jiggling lamp.

My rags, covering my body piecemeal, were dripping. My hard, bare feet, were steady on the ground. I was panting, unable to utter a word, a bitter taste in my mouth, my tongue stuck to my dirty teeth. I don't know whether the light made me look pale, but my blood seemed to want to clot in my veins. The old man, dragging his stiff leg, said to his wife:

"Bring some rum."

And turning to the girl:

"Light the stove and warm the food."

And turning to the boy:

"Put up a hammock."

To me he seemed a prodigious figure, with a broad face, skin already wrinkled, and, over his whole countenance, the reflection of an extraordinary kindness. He didn't ask who I was, what I did, why I was there. No matter what life might have taught him, he would have opened his own veins to feed one so hungry as I. He no doubt understood man's condition—and because he did he felt pity for all men alike. He came close to me, while his wife was coming back with the rum, and, taking me by the arm, said:

"My son, make yourself at home."

After I drank the rum, led by his hand, I entered a room that seemed to belong to the boy. I put on the clothes he offered me, denim trousers, a cotton shirt, and slipped into new sandals. He treated me, whom he had never seen before, like his own son. He took me into the living room, had me sit on a bench at his simple table, and served me food. The lamp was hung on the wall, by a nail. And everyone, the old man and his wife, the young girl and the boy, sat down to see me eat.

When I had finished, and as if I were in the habit of eating there every day, as if I had been born in that house and were a member of the family, the old man stood up and, turning to me, said:

"May yours be the sleep of the just."

I stayed on, living in that house, for a long time. Two years, or more. I acquired new habits, I learned to work in the cacao groves, I sensed what a mother might be like, observing how the woman treated the boy and the girl. The boy was her nephew, the girl, her daughter. How he happened to come there, whether or not he was an orphan, I never found out. He was called Mano and his sole pastime, on his days off from work, was to catch catfish in the creek. When he lay down in his hammock, which swung alongside mine, he would sleep like a rock. He seemed to love and respect no one so much as the old man, his uncle. Obedient, quiet, hard-working—such was Mano.

The girl, unobtrusive as if afraid of being seen, and humble as if afraid of offending someone, helped the mother with her housework. She always wore her red hair long, and at night, in the light, her freckles seemed more pronounced. Her eyes would open wide and gleam when the old man, having one of his heart seizures, would double forward and hold his chest with his hand. Her name was as ugly as her body, for they called her Orlandina. She appeared to know nothing of the world except that she had to do what she was doing. Except for the house, the creek, the garden in the clearing, and the sky, and except for us, no doubt everything else was empty space. The world began and ended with what she could see. Probably she believed in Itajuipe, the nearest village, because Mano always went there to buy supplies and pay taxes. I always felt that she considered me one of her father's friends and, therefore, a relative of hers. I never saw her smile, nor did I ever see her cry, not once, in all that time.

As for the older woman, her mother, shy and always pleasant, she seemed to keep belittling her own efforts. Her tone of voice was by nature low and very gentle, and, while we were having our supper, she invariably talked of the farm chores. She knew how to fry bananas, in deep fat, better than anyone I've ever known. Strong coffee she was also good at making. She only got upset when the old man, having a seizure, would cry out:

"Joana, my heart!"

She used to croon, her voice almost hushed, as if she were

lulling a child to sleep. Unlike her daughter, she never went to the vegetable patch, never helped with the cacao harvest, her longest journey being to the rocky creek, where she did her washing. She was young in spirit and some days even made jests. Like her daughter, like the boy, like me even, she made no secret of the great respect she felt in the old man's presence. Their life together, their long intimacy, had never managed to break down this distance. They understood each other, however, as if they were one person. On numbers of occasions, she suggested to me, in a whisper:

"Take good care of him. That great heart might stop," and lifting her finger to her lips, "his heart is very fragile."

I concerned myself quite a bit, during the long time I spent there, with what the old man would do should he go to the Ouro Valley. He would dominate the valley, perhaps. He would extinguish the hatred of those irascible creatures, with but a glance from his compassionate eye. He would teach beauty, finding it in the gallop of the wild horses, in the very mud of the slough, in the dusty road, in the blackness of the sky. The biting wind, which was to blame for our deep affliction, would be turned into sweet music to be heard in peace, our anger in check. When he spoke, as he did to me several times, the coarsest of men would come close, deeply touched, to listen and never to forget. Jeronimo, my poor Jeronimo, would leave his cavern, in shame. And all, in the valley, would love one another.

No force in the world could withstand his tenderness. The violence of madness and rage would be unavailing the moment his face, suddenly blanching, reflected in its immobility the great pain of one who, pardoning, could not cure. He would walk the earth naked, innocent among men, if his nakedness served to silence a blasphemy. Knowing him, I lamented myself, lamented

Jeronimo, lamented the valley. In his high-top shoes, dragging his crippled leg, a bit hunched, his hair white, in his hand a deadwood stick, old Nathanael strode the earth without any sense of possession. Whoever happened along could become its master. Once when I was arguing with Mano over who should have a hoe, he called us, quietly. And he asked, his eyes on the dewy field:

"What leads a dog, Alexandre, to dispute with another dog over a bone?"—he himself replied, his distant gaze fixed upon the dewy field—"Hunger and selfishness, Mano. Hand the hoe to Mano, Alexandre."

Lowering his voice, as we listened in silence:

"Selfishness leads a man to kill another over a piece of ground. Monstrous, this selfishness of ours."

I was amazed, at first, by Nathanael. I couldn't understand, readily, what he was saying. I well remember that once, at dinner, Mano made reference to someone who had died in Itajuipe, in the village. He put his spoon down on his plate. The girl, his daughter, bowed her head. And he observed:

"Human selfishness would be hideous if it weren't for death."

For him, it was death that gave life its permission.

It was he who, a few days after I arrived, outlining the letters in charcoal, taught me to read and write. His patience was unlimited. Of our entire group, his daughter was the only one who hadn't learned. Mano, however, had learned under him. He banished my confusion, encouraged me, repeated, went back to the beginning, repeated some more. He would say the longer words with me, syllable by syllable, as if singing. He explained, gave examples. He made me practice, asked questions, gave advice, corrected, taught. But as I overcame obstacles, step by step, now mastering reading, now laboriously writing, and when my childhood curiosity was reborn in me, the comparison that arose in my mind was not between the valley and the new land, but between Nathanael and Jeronimo. Despite all this, his extraordinary solidarity, the desire he had given me to discover things, the education that might reshape me, I preferred Jeronimo. It is hard to explain, almost impossible to give reasons, but I preferred Jeronimo.

Nathanael's greatest lesson, however, did not come from his words, but from his own actions, that is, the advocacy of goodness—which he practiced and tried to communicate—as the only vehicle capable of saving or rescuing the human race from misery. For him, had he known it or had I spoken of it, the Ouro Valley would no doubt have been an absurd fantasy. Jeronimo, a specter. Cruel and bloody images that peopled a madman's brain. His goodness stood in opposition to the valley. But the valley was in my flesh, in all that I might become, in the depths of my memory, in my blood, in my fevers. Above all, the valley had become confused with Jeronimo.

With time, while Nathanael's hair was getting whiter and his seizures were becoming shorter in duration, and while a beard was growing on Mano's face, and in the cacao groves the fruit was coming out again, came the certainty that man is always the same wherever he is. Jeronimo was capable of tearing a horse's mouth apart—but the thing that happened, in the very shadow of old Nathanael, had the end result of eliminating, in me, a great part of his influence. I can still see him, however, leaning on his walking stick, his hand reaching toward the sky.

Up high, the wind was a hand, like old Nathanael's, working the clouds. I stayed near the door, the morning well along, waiting for the sun. The rainy season was over and now, among the cacao trees, there was light. That day we had a new planting to make. The old man was still resting, Mano was sharpening his scythe. The woman had just called us to breakfast. The girl was sweeping the house. Meanwhile, since I had taken refuge there, and had been accepted like Mano himself, I had been concerned by something I had seen one night, when the deepest silence reigned, after the cock had crowed. Pretending to be asleep, I watched.

Getting out of his hammock, barefooted, Mano had opened the door, softly, with the stealth of a housebreaker. I got up a few minutes later and, with the wariness learned in the forest, I went directly to the door that led to the clearing. The latch being closed, he could not have gone out. Quickly, as never before in my life, my brain had started to move. I remembered Mano, fishing for catfish, and Orlandina, soaping clothes on the stones. Once more I could see both, in the clearing, he with the pruning hook and she with her sack, piling up the cacao pods. At table, during meals, one opposite the other. Rosalia came to mind, an unexpected apparition at that moment, and I identified myself with Mano, who was capable of attacking old Nathanael, as I had attacked Rosalia's father. Perhaps there would be a repetition, outside the valley, of what I had thought could happen only in the valley.

I almost didn't let my feet touch the ground. Holding my breath, I approached the girl's room—it was remote, near the kitchen—and, putting my ear to the door, I immediately heard Mano's voice. He was with old Nathanael's daughter, in her room. I withdrew, hurriedly, to my hammock. Wide awake, I waited for Mano to return. He came back at daybreak, as cautious as before, and lay down in his hammock. I made no move and kept my eyes shut.

It was after I had washed my face, and shaved with old Nathanael's razor, that I stood in the doorway, seeing the open sky, watching the wind, high above me, working the clouds. Mano passed by me, in silence, with his scythe in hand. The woman called us to breakfast. I even asked, precisely at the moment I was sitting down on the bench:

"Hasn't Nathanael gotten up yet?"

"He's getting up right now," replied his wife.

The girl left the room, heading for the kitchen. Unaware of me and of the world, apparently she had slept so well that one might almost say she hadn't even dreamed. Certainly no responsibility fell on her. She had felt a desire, her instinct spurring her, and she had acted. Perhaps she was unaware of her own origin and didn't suppose that she might have a baby. If her father had questioned her, she would have answered with the naturalness usual in her replies. At most, she would have run her fingers through her red hair. And she would have gone back to finish the work she had begun.

Mano, on the other hand, was frowning, and his worry was so great that no sooner had he finished breakfast than he was off to the fields. He had even forgotten to take his lunch and so Joana instructed me:

"Alexandre, you take Mano his lunch."

I was ready to leave, my knife in my belt, when old Nathanael came into the room, dragging his crippled leg. He asked me to wait, wanted to go with me so he could help a bit with the new planting. With his walking stick in one hand and the other hand resting on my shoulder, he and I entered the cacao groves. Here and there, at certain moments, the sun would shine through. We kept walking, slowly. Certain that my silence would amount to betrayal, convinced that he needed to know, I said abruptly:

"Last night Mano was in your daughter's bedroom."

Jeronimo had taught me to speak out, frankly, without wasting words. Old Nathanael, however, was not perturbed. He came to a standstill, the eye of his compassion upon me, beyond modesty and shame. On his face, the reflection of his goodness persisted. He squeezed my arm, as he always did, and said:

"The power of the flesh is greater than honor, Alexandre. It's not his fault, Alexandre. She is not to blame either."

As if nothing had happened, he kept on walking, absent-mindedly, until we came upon Mano, stripped to the waist, working the soil. He greeted the old man affably. The rest of the day we stayed there, old Nathanael sitting down most of the time, calmly directing the work. We went home at twilight, Mano ahead of us, old Nathanael seemingly tired. Opening the door, his daughter received us, her face expressionless. She kissed her father's hand, mechanically, responding to habit. And she appeared not to have seen Mano himself, because she immediately returned to the kitchen, discreetly and as quick as a wink.

It was at supper, with all of us at table, by lamplight, that old Nathanael, looking toward us—Mano and me, the girl and his wife—laid down his spoon and put his hand over his plate. The peacefulness of his gaze, more profound than ever before, was strangely moving. His lips showed no tremor and his hair shone in the light. He was not going to scold, one could see from his serenity. He was not going to give orders, one could guess. Mano waited. The woman waited. I too waited. Only his daughter seemed not to understand matters. After a fraction of a second, and when his voice was about to make itself heard, Mano anticipated him and, calmly, without affectation, said:

"She is like my sister, Uncle, but she will be my wife."

"All right," the old man replied, "let us now hasten the wedding day."

And everyone there, suddenly, felt happy. Everyone, except the girl. Alien to what was going on, she continued to seem far away. Remotely, perhaps she understood—she was going to belong to Mano just as her mother belonged to her father. Or perhaps, inwardly out of place in the outer world, she understood nothing at all. It was even likely that the meaning of the word "wedding" escaped her. Mano did not seek her with his eyes— that would have been useless effort. The old man, ever tranquil, continued:

"The first thing in the morning"—and he turned to Mano— "you will go to the village. We must see to everything."

I feared the village of Itajuipe, my painful impression of the village of Coaraci still vivid. Brought together, in a group, men turn cruel and lose the kindliness I had known, in the countryside, at old Nathanael's. They all went, but I stayed behind. While waiting for their return, at the mercy of the past, which was becoming more poignant, I kept trying to understand whether the Ouro Valley had moved farther away or had remained, alive within me, like a sinister attraction. As powerful as ever, without slipping an inch—the image of Jeronimo. I did some worrying about what people might have done to the land that belonged to me. Had my house been set afire? My crops put to the torch? My livestock spared? Were the gallows still maintained, upraised, in expectation? Immediate reality, however, rose up in formidable opposition. Old Nathanael stood out like a tremendous human bulwark, influencing, demonstrating that I could no longer return to my past. Soon, we would have a baby in the house. "The child!" I murmured.

In the valley, the child of a man and a woman does not awaken joy. It is put down on the ground, with the dogs. It grows up, as Rosalia did, running against the wind, aggressiveness early written on its face, its tormented gaze reflecting the somber sky. Despised by the mother. Cuffed by the father. Its brother is an enemy no less harsh than the earth. "The child!"—I heard, with amazement but without horror, in Nathanael's now silent house, Rosalia's terrible cry. Her child did not achieve life, and if it had, would its destiny have been different from my own? Had it been weak, it would have died from its own weakness; strong, like Jeronimo, it would have been an unfinished monster.

Outside the valley, however, a child was awaited just as people looked forward to harvest day. There is tenderness to shelter it, love to protect it, and the demand for submissiveness is veiled. In sickness, it is comforted by the climate of kindness. Quite often, it becomes the justification for life itself. As a compensation, above all as a recompense for doing good, old Nathanael and his wife—the stout and smiling Joana—would gentle their old age laughing at their grandchild's laughter. It would not be long in coming, that was sure. And it would be healthy, rosy-cheeked, beautiful.

More observant than the father, that same Mano who had become transfigured with the prospect of the child—able to make a joke now and to be more friendly—I could see, day by day, the enormous transformation in his wife. Her hair was still worn loose. Her gaze still seemed far away. But, without having reached the point of excitement, she displayed a different temperament. She did not laugh, as she used to, nor cry, as always before. Rather, she now enjoyed a certain mastery over the outside world, with heightened awareness, a somewhat lessened insensitivity, and the ability to participate in conversations.

Around her, there was created an atmosphere so soft and delicate that one might have compared it to wool.

Joana, the future grandmother, showed us the things she had sewed. I myself helped Mano build a cradle. Old Nathanael, seeking me out, told me I would be the godfather. And, seizing the opportunity, he enlightened me, firmly:

"We are always rewarded when we are good."

Vaguely, though without grief or resentment, I would compare Mano's wife to Rosalia, Rosalia's child to her child, their house to my house. In the valley, such a life would have been unthinkable. The crazy wind would already have banished joy; a man chastised in his soul could not recover his calm without bitterness. Like old Nathanael, like the father himself, and as if I had not come from the Ouro Valley, I too was looking forward to Mano's child as to a gift for those who do no one harm, for the humble and selfless who sacrifice themselves for the love of their fellow men. Without having a right to happiness, as he did —the human climate was so gentle that I believed in the child as in a force capable of accomplishing, within me, a great inner reform.

With the birth of the child—I thought to myself—the valley would die.

It was Joana, Nathanael's wife, who went running at the first groan. There was not time for Mano to go to the village to get the midwife. In the kitchen, at Joana's bidding, Mano was boiling the water. Old Nathanael, in the bedroom, was assisting his daughter. As always happened under any strong emotional stress, I thought of Jeronimo. Had he been there, chewing his wad of tobacco, perhaps he would have crossed his arms on his mighty chest. Perhaps he would have looked with indifference at the morning light now invading the house, lifting the fields out of the foggy shadows. It was a warm, valley morning—I remembered, as I waited, isolated and useless, for Mano or old Nathanael to call me—and as soon as Jeronimo had fed the fire more wood, someone pounded on the cavern door, shouting.

The eternal wind whipped the leafless branches, picked up dust from the road, and whirled along furiously castigating the valley. Jeronimo opened the door, the wind devastating the cavern, and let in Gabino, the horsebreaker. He was a short, thickset man, who lived nearby with his wife, at the edge of the open prairie. Like almost everyone else in the valley, he lived to himself with his animals. He came in and announced:

"My wife is feeling very bad. She's ready to have her baby. She's about to die with groaning, but the baby won't come out.

And he said, in a loud voice, to overcome the force of the wind:

"I would like to ask your help."

In what way Jeronimo might help, I had no idea. I went along, at a run, for my short boyish legs could not keep up with his hurrying stride. When the open prairie came into view, you could see Gabino's place. A house with two rooms, living room and kitchen, but stoutly constructed—people always built thus in the valley—set firmly in the ground, capable of meeting the storms and the constant wind. The woman was moaning, her belly huge, as she lay on the oxhide. Whether because of an Indian custom he had learned or because he had once observed it there in the valley, Jeronimo picked the woman up in his robust arms and ordered Gabino to bring the hide. He stopped under a clump of trees, with low-hanging, leafless branches. Gabino set the hide on the ground, as if it were a sheet. The woman was sweating, her lips trembling, her eyes those of a frightened animal. Setting her on her feet, he fastened her hands around a branch, supporting her body himself. The wind was blinding and hurt your skin. The woman made herself contract, her neck veins bulging, until blood was followed by flesh in the form of a human, ever so tiny, that Jeronimo cut free. Then it started wailing.

Then, brusquely interrupting my memory, startling me, Mano's voice as I had never heard it before:

"Alexandre!"

I was in the bedroom in a second, but, when I looked at old Nathanael and saw his face as white as his hair, his lips retracted as if attempting to say something, his gaze fastened upon the bed, I could immediately see that his case was hopeless. Mano, overwhelmed by the fantastic apparition, had tears in his eyes. Joana, her hands vile with blood, was leaning against the wall to keep from falling. I drew near, in silence, seeking the cause. I could make out the woman, in bed, lost to reality, her red hair framing a face without pain. Beside her, naked and breathing, was something that might have been a human being—but was actually a horrible mass, its mouth a huge gash, its forehead sunken, lacking arms, its feet without toes, its eyes blind. It was alive, however. I could still hear, as an order, the terrifying voice of Jeronimo: "Strangle the monster, Alexandre. Throw the monster to the pigs!" I was going to do it, was opening my hands to do it when old Nathanael's arm arose and his clenched hand, jerking and tremulous, went to his heart. Like a hook, it clutched his flesh. He dropped his head, gasping, and his great heart shattered like glass.

I saw no more, I heard no more, whether earth rose up or the heavens fell, whether there were tears or screams, curses or silence—mute, deaf, and blind, once again cut asunder from every-

thing and everybody, I saw the Ouro Valley, like a sinister glow-
ing torch, violent and strange, reappearing before me. Its wind
lashed out and grew into a deep roar. In a stampede, their manes
flowing, its wild horses bolted. The mud of the slough bubbled
like molten lava. The nubs of the leper's unspeakable hands became one with the cactus. Towering over me, reaching beyond
the mountains and the forests, came the image of Jeronimo. He
called to me, shouting, like a man possessed. The fire in his cavern was blazing before my eyes. And, finally, with a whir like an
immense lasso, the raving wind furiously dragged me away.

I turned my back on the room and went out the door, with no
other wrap than the clothes on my body, already dazzled by the
vision of the harsh and indomitable valley that awaited me.

It was as if there was no one left behind me. Expelled as from
a cloud of smoke into a devastated landscape, I do not know
even now how my hands endured, and my legs, and my brain. If
there was suffering, I did not feel it. Images and sensations, all
inner movement shattered like pent-up waters, suddenly released, that inundate and drown. Lucidity, at rare moments,
would surface, but immediately everything would turn into the
wind that was pulling me, tugging me—I, a phantom, without
flesh, blood, life. It was not a journey but a wingless flight. Men
or animals, swamps or stones—I did not encounter them. Under
the spell of the valley, everyday reality was sacrificed.

When I once more became aware, first of the horrid light, then
of my strangling thirst, finally of a numbing physical ache, I set
out, my body a single wound, in search of water to slake my
thirst and relieve my pain. I had tried to drink the light—bright,
dry, pitiless—but I took in air, filling my lungs to the fullest, and
it was as if I could already see myself in front of the fire, in Je-

ronimo's cavern. This was valley air. I raised my head, seeking the sky. There it was, black and heavy. Violent blasts of wind enveloped me, curing my body, making it strong. My foot came down on a hot straight line, the dust rose, it was the road. I lay down and waited for night, the great night of the valley.

I got up in the dark, the valley asleep. I could see nothing around me but the night. As I walked, I could hear nothing but the wind. The night, the wind, I—the valley would have consisted of nothing more were it not for the emergence in the dark of an even darker point, Jeronimo's cavern. Without emotion, without hurrying, I rapped on the door. I waited, not shouting. When it opened, the wind entering with me, night remaining outside, I saw Jeronimo.

And from Jeronimo I heard the question I had not expected: "Why did you come back?"

DOWN THERE IN THE VALLEY, let this echo fade that belongs not to me but to the wind that encircles us, like invisible combatants, on this piece of ground. Everyone, this moment, flee. I no longer need human ears, I can dispense with compassion and pity. Let everyone stand back. These mute walls—let them come down with a roar. Put out the lantern. Let light shine, with the break of day, and confirm in the valley the wrath of the valley. Jeronimo, I know, will arrive too late.

Now, there is only that marvelous road, the road that cannot be compared to the road in the valley, but the road that opens, before my eyes, at a sign from Abilio, my father. I see him, ahead there, guiding me. All around, the rest is blackness. My poor heart can no longer see, my hands are useless—there is no more pain from the wounds in my body. My brain forms no questions, my tongue is not speaking. But my feet keep on walking, ever so slowly.

It is possible that the living can no longer reach me. Silently, like doomed specters homeless among the worlds, it is possible that the dead have spied me. Rosalia, whom I cannot see. Nathanael, whom I cannot hear. Paula, whom I did not know. Let them observe, in expectation, but without anxiety. I shall reach them, in a few minutes, because the road that takes me is not long and infinite like the road in the valley.

My feet slip, my body falls, my mouth giving no cry. The final air is foul. The mud that absorbs me, and asphyxiates me, in the slough, is viscous. With a lightning suddenness, the valley and the wind are hidden. Everything comes to a close, gradually, with serenity and immense quietude.

Lightning Source UK Ltd.
Milton Keynes UK
UKOW04f2131080917
308750UK00001B/104/P